RANCH-HAND WOLF'S AFFAIR

PARANORMAL TRUE MATE DATING AGENCY

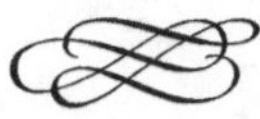

AMELIA WILSON

SSPATEL PUBLISHING

CONTENTS

PROLOGUE: DANVER

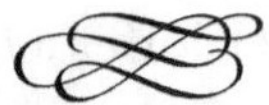

1992: Suburban Wisconsin

Danver Collins finally had everything he had always dreamed of. He was a well-respected member of his suburb, despite being a werewolf. In fact, many of his neighbors were members of the area's pack, which had insinuated itself perfectly into the cute little cluster of neighborhoods outside of Madison, Wisconsin.

The humans didn't know he was a werewolf, of course, but they liked him enough to elect him President of the HOA. He'd campaigned for months and now, finally, he could do his best for the community, blissfully ignorant humans and friendly werewolves alike.

Danver loved the neighborhood and everything it stood for: peace, family, and security. He was especially glad to be able to improve it because . . . his wife was currently pregnant with their first son. She was four months pregnant. The bump was already showing quite a bit on her lean frame. Danver thought she looked more beautiful than ever, and told her so every day, even though the back pain and nausea made her scowl at him.

She was another wolf, and it was generally very hard for werewolf females to conceive. It was as if werewolf sperm didn't want to mate with their own kind. That was why many werewolf males sought out human females, which Danver thought was a dangerous practice.

What if the woman you seduced didn't want to mate with someone outside of her species? And even if she did, how could you be confident of her loyalty when you became the target of an angry mob or "supers", the killers who hunted supernatural beings?

At least vampires could turn their lovers and offer them immortal life. What could a werewolf male offer a human female, besides a mate and children who would outlive her?

Danver was young and blond and many people told him he could be an actor. He had the chiseled jaw, flexing muscles, and height for the job. He would be a shoo-in for the All-American super hero part. He was more than happy with Esther, his wife, who, despite having an odd, old-fashioned name, was a beautiful woman. She was tall, almost as tall as Danver, and blonde as he was. She was like a living sculpture, a great work of art.

The mean, jealous women in the neighborhood called her Barbie when they thought Danver wasn't listening. Of course, they had no way of knowing that the level of his hearing was supernaturally good.

He had been mated to Esther for eight years only, hardly any time at all for a werewolf, but he knew Esther was deeply devoted to him. Having a family was all they ever talked about. Sure, sometimes she'd start asking why the heck they lived in Wisconsin, when they could live anywhere in the world, but he had made it clear – he couldn't leave the pack.

Danver just wasn't the type of wolf who could abandon the community he'd come to love. He thought they loved him, too. He worked as an actuary in a local insurance firm. It was good work for him. He felt as if he was helping people while making the cogs of society continue to whir. He tried to be home every day by five o'clock, without fail. He wanted to set a good precedent of being there in the evenings to take over childcare from his wife. She'd handle the days, when he was gone to work, and he'd take over at night.

He was so excited to be having a child that he didn't doubt at all that he would be able to handle the kids after work. Werewolves have incredible stamina. The little plights and dramas of Corporate America didn't wear him not down, not when he considered the growing family he had to support.

Of course, he was an able-bodied werewolf male. He was excited to come home for more than one reason. He knew Esther took her nap about this time. She slept in the nude. The thought of it made him start to feel more animal, even as he kept his hands carefully on the wheel at ten and two.

He thought about her beautiful thighs, rubbing against each other roughly, as she slept and dreamed. He always asked what she was dreaming of, but she never answered, as if it was too dirty to share. He was fine with keeping it a mystery; it was more exciting that way.

Plus, if she felt like she couldn't tell him something, he trusted her judgment. Everyone needs their little secrets, he supposed. As long as they weren't too hurtful.

Lost in imaginings of his wife's naked body writhing sweatily on their sheets, and just waiting to be satisfied by him, he found that he had absentmindedly pulled into their neighborhood without registering the journey. He'd have to pay better attention. Even a werewolf's quick reflexes were pressed at freeway speeds, especially if he was daydreaming and distracting himself.

He walked up the stone walkway, full of nice river rocks he'd gathered and set himself. It was lined with little sunflowers he'd planted, so you walked up to the door on a winding trail of pretty rocks and flowers smiling at you.

When he took out his keys to enter the door, he heard his wife's dreamy groaning from upstairs, and smiled.

Then the keys fell out of his hands. Because his wife wasn't the only one he could hear groaning. Not bothering to pick up his keys, he made a fist and drove it straight through their door, breaking it off the hinges. He tossed the door to the side and ran upstairs.

He was so fast no one would have had a chance to stop what they were doing. So, when he threw open the door to the bedroom, he got an eyeful of something he wished every day afterwards that he could unsee.

His beautiful, normally dignified wife was positioned in doggy style, her ass up and her face grinding into their bedsheets. Behind her was a scrawny human male that Danver didn't recognize at first. The guy was driving his hips and cock so deeply into Danver's wife that his penis completely disappeared inside of her and didn't come back out.

They were groaning, huffing and puffing as if they were getting a good workout. It was so mechanical and impersonal that Danver's brain had a hard time recognizing it as sex for a minute.

The human male had his hands splayed wide on Esther's ass, gripping her cheeks to pull her toward his thrusting hips as hard as possible. He had his eyes closed, and Esther's face was mashed into the bed. As he fucked her, he drove her body harder into the bed.

He reached up and smacked her ass while calling her a filthy slut. She squealed. Danver couldn't tell if it was a happy noise or a reaction to pain. The sound was so strange to his ears . . . he'd never heard her made a sound like that.

But the sound of someone calling his wife a slut was too much to take. Danver leaped forward and in three steps, he was across the bedroom and on top of the bed with the human male's throat in his hands.

He pressed him against the wall, his toes barely on the bed. The human male panicked, screaming for Danver to let him go. Danver leaned really close to his face and growled violently.

Esther screamed and tried to pull Danver off the male. She was also trying to cover herself, as if her modesty could be preserved by a bedsheet at this juncture. She wasn't able to get enough leverage though, and Danver tightened his grip on the male, leaning in to menace him.

Danver bared his teeth and roared. The man started to cry. Danver recognized him as the local school's principal, and another member of the HOA. Once he realized that, he noticed that the man's toupee was slipping off his sweaty head, as well. He threw him off the bed. The man shouted out in pain and shock, but he got to his feet and looked at Danver in absolute fear.

Danver growled, "Get out."

The man said, "Yeah, sorry," and ran for his life.

As Esther cried on the bed, all of the energy suddenly went out of Danver. He looked at her, feeling almost sleepy. He hoped she was sorry enough for him to forgive her.

Instead, she screamed, "You could have killed him, you idiot."

With a big huff of rage, she rolled off the bed and grabbed a robe. Danver got up and mindlessly went downstairs to pour himself a glass of milk. He sat at the table.

Esther joined him, saying derisively, "A warm glass of milk. Are you a baby?"

Danver was confused. He couldn't bring himself to say anything, but he felt as if she was being overly aggressive, for someone who should be begging for forgiveness. It was as if she was mad he dared to catch her cheating on him.

The next conversation was very one-sided. The truth poured out of Esther, at first spitefully, but then she cried and hid her face. This life they were building together was too dull. It was unnatural for werewolves to live in such calm, civilized circumstances. Esther missed hunting, fighting . . . wildness.

Danver wasn't exactly sure how that translated into mediocre sex with a balding school administrator, but she explained, saying that having an affair, though a banal suburban thing in itself, was the only way she could get the excitement back into her sex life. She told Danver it was his fault. He was too considerate a lover, and there was no excitement in sleeping with him; not after eight years. Sex with him was good enough, but there was no danger.

He nodded. That was fair. He always liked his partners to feel safe and cared for, even when things got a little rough. She saw him nod, and it infuriated her more. She threw a glass at his head. He reached up to catch it, but he only managed to bat it into the floor, where it shattered loudly.

Something came to mind that suddenly became the most important thing in Danver's universe.

He asked, "How long?"

She choked out, "Four months." After a lengthy pause, during which Danver wished God would strike him down with a thunderbolt, she finally admitted, "It's his baby. Not yours."

He said, "How do you know?"

She looked him dead in the eye. "Counting. I conceived with him, not with you."

Without another word, Danver got up, walked out of the house, and tore up every damn flower he'd ever planted. Then he got into his car and drove away, swearing that no matter what else he did in his lifetime, he wouldn't give someone else this pain. He'd never tear apart a family.

And he was never tempted to do it.

Until after several decades of roaming the country, lonely and grieving, he joined a new pack. There he met Melanie, who was more of a woman than he'd ever dreamed of.

But . . . she had a husband and son, already. And although Danver thought about her constantly, and her husband was a scrub, he would never come between them. Not even if it was all that Danver and Melanie wanted in this world.

MELANIE

*H*er little pack was enjoying a picnic out on the ranch. Melanie stood under the shade of a huge, old tree. Shade was rare in the desert, but it was well into autumn now and the temperatures were perfect for lovely days outside with the little ones.

In her mind, her son Michael was still a little one, which was not at all true. He'd been scrawny, a runt of his "litter" (what a bigger pack called a generation of wolf pups. Although the women only had one wolf at a time, the kids were generally raised communally). Then his growth spurt had hit. When they'd moved out to New Mexico, a year ago, to live with Melanie's brother, Wes, and his new pack, her son had gotten much bigger and much surlier. He was as tall as Carl, who was 6'5", and thick like Wes, who looked like he could run into a brick wall and bring it down. It was still weird to her; Michael had always been a skinny kid.

The funny thing was he looked so much like Wes, except he never smiled. If it weren't for the frown, Michael would look like her brother's clone, which made sense. People usually thought Wes and Melanie were twins. They all had the same olive-to-tan skin, big face-filling smiles, and striking dark eyes. Except her son refused to smile. Oh well, teenagers are going to do their thing.

She watched her brother clap a hand on Michael's back and make a joke. Michael ripped his shoulder away and walked off, pretending to get a drink, but really snubbing his Uncle.

Last year, after Michael's maturation ceremony, Wes had stolen his new car and totaled it. Michael was still pissed about that, and that his uncle was the reason they had moved from Washington to New Mexico.

Oh well. Nothing to do about it, the kid was sure to be pissed after they moved him away from all his friends. He'd understand why this was the right pack for them when he was older.

She looked at Wes's mate, Cassidy, chasing their little baby around and playing tag. Cassidy refused to play hide and seek after the baby had been kidnapped last year. Wes had rescued him with the help of another pack member (the only one who wasn't related to Melanie), Danver Collins. Danver was a good guy, if Melanie had ever seen one, and he had a superhero's physique to boot.

Her nephew Davie was really a baby, but he was getting bigger every day, it seemed. At three years old, he was a toddling pup who was learning how to control his strengths and powers. Well, starting to learn.

It was kind of funny to watch his mom, Cassidy, freak out about stuff that was normal for werewolf pups. Such as how he kept hunting small insects and lizards and devouring them. Melanie figured that was unsettling for human mothers, but she and Wes just kept explaining to her that Davie needed to learn how to hunt, just as much as he needed to learn to read.

Melanie just said with a sigh, "Thank goodness I have wolves here. If I was raising him on my own, I'd be as confused as all hell. It's not as if 'how to raise a werewolf baby' is easy to Google."

Looking at her own son standing by himself by the soda cooler, Melanie thought about how there was no instruction manual for relationships either. For instance, she was discouraging the pack calling her husband, who had disappeared after what was supposed to be a quick visit to his relatives in Washington. He was only supposed to be away for three days, but now it had been three weeks.

Melanie should be scared, except it wasn't the first time. Carl lost his phone and did shit like that all the time. But three weeks was pretty long, even for him.

Carl didn't like Wes. Carl didn't like New Mexico. Sometimes Melanie thought the only thing Carl liked was video games and energy drinks. He was kind of a strange wolf. Most wolves loved being outdoors and getting fresh air and exercise. Carl wasn't really that kind of lupine.

Melanie had been fine with it for a long time. In Washington, it was so gloomy out, and she wanted her son to focus on school rather than wolf stuff anyway. But now that they were out in New Mexico, with Wes and Danver as role models for her son, showing him what a grown shifter male should be like, she'd gotten more and more short-tempered with her layabout, gamer husband.

So his "short trips to see relatives" got longer and longer. This was the longest yet. Three weeks, and he'd barely called at all. And he wasn't picking up his phone.

She stood under the tree and listened to the phone ring for way too long. It clicked off. It didn't even go to voicemail.

Melanie didn't put her phone away. She needed a moment of peace to control her emotions.

She loved Carl. They'd been together for three decades, and they hadn't expected to be able to conceive. Michael had been a complete surprise and a blessing. She'd thought it was a sign that she'd found the right mate. It was difficult to find two werewolves who were biologically compatible enough to conceive. When she thought about how lucky she was to find someone like that, she'd always felt as if she was walking on cloud nine.

But now Michael was nearly grown, and all he wanted to do was play Call of Whatever and glare at the rest of the pack. He only wanted to be around his dad. And his dad only wanted to be back in Washington, sitting inside with his family, playing games. His dad definitely didn't want to pick up a phone call from his mom, apparently. This time they'd really have to talk about it. Melanie hadn't been saying anything about his long trips. After all, she'd uprooted his life when she's asked to move to New Mexico.

But this was ridiculous. Three weeks of abandoning his family just to goof around with his brothers, all of whom were wastes of space, anyway. Not one of them had a job; they just hunted occasionally to keep the pack from kicking them out.

Melanie determined that as soon as he got back, Carl would either start have to helping on the ranch, or get a job. If he didn't want to work outside as the rest of them did, keeping the ranch self-sustainable for the most part and selling at farmers markets, then he could earn his keep some other way. It was only fair, and Melanie's patience had run out.

She slipped her phone back into her pocket, her tears at being abandoned transmuted into rage, which she felt way more comfortable with. She walked over to the picnic table, where Danver was passing out the main course. He'd grilled some delicious burgers for everybody, and every ingredient came from the family ranch (which made Melanie a lot more squeamish than it made the werewolves . . . They understood there was no life for prey without predators, but there were also no predators without prey, and you had to respect the balance).

Her family greeted her with smiles, except for her sullen son, but she didn't care. Everyone's smiles and the sight of him, so safe and loved in his new pack, made her happy anyway. If Carl didn't appreciate what he had, he'd lose it. She made that promise to herself as she tore into the burger Danver handed her. It was absolutely delicious.

She fluttered her eyelashes at him. It was impossible not to flirt with the guy. He was so hot, and it embarrassed him so much to be hit on.

She said, "Wow, and you can cook, too?"

He suppressed a smile and said, "Call it a necessary skill for a bachelor."

He liked to point out that he was the only unattached member of the pack. He'd helped Wes and Melanie rescue Davie, after he'd been kidnapped by rival werewolves in the area (who were no longer a problem, AKA dead as doornails), a year ago. After that, he'd become an adopted but very official member of their pack.

Melanie watched his heroic, muscly torso move. She'd thought she'd met hot werewolves before, but this guy really took the cake. He had on overalls but no T-shirt underneath, so you could see wisps of golden chest hair and the perfect hard surface of his pecs. What a tease. Melanie imagined yet again what he looked like stripped down and smacked around a bit. He was such a calm guy . . .

What did he act like when he got really riled up? She'd pay good money to see that show. Or maybe she was just a lonely, horny house-wife, she thought bitterly.

When Carl got back, they were going to have some big, big talks.

DANVER

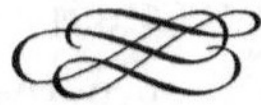

*D*anver wished Melanie's beauty would lessen over time. But every time he saw her walk into a room, or saw her smile burst out in its gorgeous fireworks display over her face, the fire erupted from his chest and from . . . the lower regions.

He tried not to be alone with her. He knew his feelings for her were totally inappropriate. And he wished Carl wasn't dumb enough to spend so much time away from her. How could you tear yourself away from a woman like that? Carl must have seen how men came to heel at Melanie's command so easily. Whenever they were in town, all she had to do was blink her pretty eyes and men were falling over themselves to do her favors, give her free stuff, buy the ranch's goods, you name it.

Danver had asked once, very stupidly, how she did it. If it was some kind of pheromone or something she was putting out. She had grinned and laughed at him. She leaned close to him and asked, "What do you think it is?"

He looked at her luscious lips and long, black lashes. He tried not to look at the gorgeous curve of her breasts peeking out of the top of her blouse.

He couldn't come up with an answer that didn't totally reveal how much he wanted to throw her onto the farmers' market table and take her, propriety be damned. So he just shrugged and walked away, even though he knew that was rude. Better to be rude, so he had no chance of her falling for him in return.

He sat in the living room with Wes, chatting about the pack's plans for the next day. It'd be another early wake-up on the ranch, but Danver didn't mind. Putting in a hard day's work meant a good night's sleep.

He had to utterly exhaust himself so his body would forget Melanie was sleeping alone all these nights, in the bedroom next to his. It had now been a month since her husband had left. Danver didn't have to imagine how lonely and forgotten Melanie must feel, despite the brave face she put on everything.

Danver and Wes went over the work that had to be done the next day (they argued as usual about how much really needed to be done – Wes wasn't lazy, per se – just more relaxed than Danver about things); Melanie and Cassidy walked down the stairs and passed the living room sharing smiles.

Melanie said, "Goddamn, Cassidy, that baby of yours is too cute."

Cassidy laughed. "The only thing he got from me is his hair color. Besides that, he looks just like you and Wes."

Melanie waved her off. "No, Wes isn't that cute. Definitely gets his good looks from you."

This gratified Cassidy. Melanie and her sister-in-law got along perfectly well, which was a blessing for the pack's cohesion. With such a small group, only five adults and two pups (it was hard to think of Cassidy's teenage son as a real adult, he never took his earbuds out or stopped scowling); it was good that they got along so well.

They went into the kitchen to share a drink and a chat. Danver couldn't help but tune out from what Wes was saying and tune into Melanie's voice. She had a light, dancing style of speaking, graceful but husky and deep. She sounded like a singer. When they were in wolf form, helping toddler Davie get used to changing and feeling comfortable in his wolf body, during a full moon, Melanie's gorgeously toned howl sent shivers up and down Danver's back. Her voice in any form had the clearest, boldest tones and was incredibly alluring.

She and Cassidy were talking about what they usually talked about at the end of the day, once they'd covered all their worries and celebrations about the kids. Where the hell was Carl?

Cassidy said with trepidation, "Is it time to get worried yet, or . . . ?"

Melanie huffed. "No. What trouble could he have got into? He doesn't have anything anybody wants. He doesn't carry money or valuables. Plus, he's a werewolf, who is staying with a family of werewolves. No, he's safe and sound. He's just choosing not to come home. He's found something... more important to do, than be here with me and Michael."

Danver's heart pulsed with a violent pain at the thought. Michael was a surly kid, but he was going through a challenging time in wolf development. He needed his father to guide him through the changes, which were much more aggressive than regular human puberty.

It was doubly hard for him, because Melanie didn't want to home-school him. She wanted him to have a chance to meet other kids outside of the homestead, as the pack was so small. This was hard, because he'd only ever had to socialize with other werewolf kids before, when they were back in Seattle.

Danver understood the choice, and he knew that Michael wouldn't appreciate being homeschooled, but Michael didn't appreciate anything about his new life. Danver understood that, too. The kid was a hundred times stronger than the other kids in his class; but, he had to learn how to hide it so no one got suspicious. Not to mention it was impossible to keep up with the hair growth at that age. You couldn't control it yet, and neither could a razor.

Melanie's thoughts were going in the same direction. She said quietly, so that Michael wouldn't hear from the upstairs, if he was still awake, "I think the worst part is that Michael clearly blames me. It's not like I can argue with him and tell him his Dad just doesn't give a damn anymore. Maybe he never did."

Her voice got very, very quiet at the end of her sentence, which even Danver, relatively new to her life, knew meant she was trying not to cry.

Cassidy, who was an empathetic human, asked, "How are you feeling?"

Melanie laughed, a breathy, weak thing. She said, "Honestly? Horny. Horny as hell. Like I need an excessively good fuck. I need a spiritual-level banging."

Cassidy laughed with her and said, "Yeah, we've all been there."

Melanie said, "I can't believe you spent two years on your own with Davie. How did you deal with it? The loneliness. Also, how did you not kill my brother when he showed up again?"

Cassidy hemmed and hawed, and tried to put off the question. Danver got nervous. Was she going to admit how they'd all met?

She was. He cringed as she said, "Honestly, I was fine for a long time. Until Davie was kidnapped and then I realized I needed help. I needed family, affection, other adults . . . Nothing wrong with needing support."

He breathed deeply in relief. Maybe she wouldn't mention the dating service . . .

Danver wondered about himself, not for the first time since Melanie had showed up. Was he worried about Cassidy revealing the truth of how they'd met, because he was embarrassed about it, or because he didn't want Melanie to know about the Dating Agency? Because, then she might . . . use it.

Melanie didn't let it lie. She asked, "But how did you contact Wes? And how the heck did you both meet Danver? You've all been kind of . . . unclear on all of that."

Cassidy laughed nervously. "It's kind of silly. Have you ever heard of the Paranormal True Mate Dating Agency?"

Danver's heart dropped. So, it was out on the table now. Melanie would know he was Cassidy's reject, sent by a dating agency for werewolves.

Melanie hadn't heard of it. Cassidy explained, and as they giggled over the scandalous nature of the organization, she even pulled up the website to show Melanie.

Cassidy said, "You fill out one of their forms, describing yourself and what you're looking for. Then, you pick whether you want one or two wolves . . . I picked two." Melanie hooted at that. Cassidy continued, "After you submit, they match you up with potentially perfect mates. Then they send them to you for a trial period."

They looked up and down the site together. Melanie said, "Okay, this is great, but this page is for human women. Is there a section for wolves to apply?" They explored the site a bit and giggled over a blog about human and werewolf pleasure. Apparently, werewolf men needed a lot of explanations about the g-spot and how to avoid tearing their partner apart, literally rather than figuratively.

Wes flicked Danver on the side of the head. Danver glared at him and growled.

Wes said, "Bro, don't eat me. I was just trying to get your attention. You've been spaced out for the last ten minutes. I said we should put wings on the cows and push them off the roof of the barn so they could learn to fly, and you said that sounds good."

Danver grunted and turned away. He said grumpily, "Half the stuff that comes out of your mouth is so ridiculous. I guess I've stopped being able to tell what's a joke and what's not."

Wes said, "Everything I say is a joke, but that doesn't stop you from telling me I'm an idiot. Where's your mind at, man?"

Danver didn't know how to answer that. Because he was listening to Wes's sister exploring a dating site. She'd found the page where werewolf women could build their profile and she was answering the questions about her ideal mate.

Danver couldn't take it. He excused himself from the conversation with Wes and walked into the kitchen. Melanie and Cassidy looked up at him and waved, but then they both paused at the strained look on his face. Cassidy started to ask him what was wrong, but he didn't let her finish the question.

He said to Melanie, feeling as if he could barely control his voice, "Where on that form are you going to tell them you already have a mate?"

Melanie held his gaze. She was never the type to back down or scare easy. Her beautiful eyes locked with his and thrilled him, even as he felt torn up by what was happening.

That hadn't been what he wanted to say. He wanted to tell her she was beautiful and deserved more than the Paranormal True Mate Dating Agency would ever provide. He wanted to offer to provide it.

But he couldn't do that. He couldn't be the one who separated a family.

It would be so painful to watch some other strange wolf come in and wreck any chance of Melanie reconciling with Carl. There could be an explanation. Or maybe he could be made to see what a colossal idiot he was being.

Melanie said sternly, "Do you see my mate anywhere around here?" He couldn't answer. He wanted to say yes and volunteer for the role himself, but the words never came.

Melanie turned back to the form with a sigh. Cassidy put her hand on her back. Danver felt like an idiot for butting in at all.

Then Melanie turned to him with a little less rage in her deep-set eyes. She said, "I'll explain the situation to the wolf they send. But I can't spend all my time wishing my mate would come home. Maybe if he's worried about losing me, Carl will stick around next time." She held her stoic expression for a second, but then her face fell, and she hid behind her hands.

She admitted shakily, "I know he has . . . someone else, in Seattle. He's been with someone else. I saw his texts to her on his phone when he was here last. He's probably with her right now."

Cassidy scooted closer and held Melanie as her chest shook, tears threatening to fall any second.

Danver murmured, "I'm sorry," and escaped out the front door. As quickly as he could manage, he shifted. He needed to hunt. He needed blood and violence to distract him from how much he wanted to rip Carl's throat out. He wasn't sure how he would respond if the ungrateful lech ever did come home.

Danver got the scent of a deer on the wind, and took off at full speed, without hesitation. He had to get away from Melanie's intoxicating smell and his desperate urge to take her into his arms and satiate every emotional and physical need she's ever had.

He wondered if he could get away whenever the Paranormal True Mate Dating Agency . . . candidate . . . arrived. Perhaps it was time for a vacation. Perhaps it was time to leave this adopted pack for good, and seek out his own true mate.

MELANIE

Melanie felt a little ridiculous. She'd always thought of herself as a very mature wolf for her age. She'd done the responsible thing and handled her own shit for literally her whole life. So why the hell was she wearing a dress and waiting for a blind date with a stranger she was matched with online? This felt anything but responsible.

At least she'd been smart enough not to put in the pack's home address as the meeting place. She was meeting the guy in the open air, in a city park in one of the little towns they went to for farmers markets. She hadn't given her last name or any information really that would identify her if the meeting went poorly, or if she changed her mind.

She doubted this decision every moment. When she thought of the texts on Carl's phone, she felt more resolved than ever to have some fun of her own. Then she'd think of how hurt Danver had looked when he'd overheard them filling out her profile . . .

Why the hell did she feel upset that Danver didn't want her messing around while her husband was gone? Like she was hurting him somehow? He was being a sanctimonious ass, sticking his nose into her business, like he stuck his nose into everyone's personal

19

affairs. She tried to explain it away, but still, she couldn't stop feeling like . . . as if she wanted to call the whole thing off and go and tell Danver she'd changed her mind. But changed it to what?

She reminded herself that she didn't owe anybody anything. She'd given Carl years and a child and, still, he'd abandoned her. She barely knew Danver.

She allowed the nervousness to turn into excitement. She thought about her answers to the profile quiz on the agency's website. She'd asked for someone fun and adventurous, who loved the great outdoors, but who also appreciated the finer things in life, such as good wine and excellent art.

It was a high bar to meet. She realized that. But she figured if she was going this far out on a limb, it was better to ask for a perfect wolf than sell herself short.

It was cold out. Not that werewolves were affected by temperatures as easily as humans were, but they had to dress the part, after all. So Melanie was wearing black tights with a tight little dress, and a big coat so she'd look insulated like the human females walking in the park. It was a funny thing about living in the desert of New Mexico instead of the forests of Washington – in Seattle, you could walk around all year, even when it was coldest, in shorts and a T-shirt. Natives did that. Here, if it dipped below 80 Fahrenheit and you weren't wearing at least a cardigan, you stood out like a sore thumb. One of the impressive things about humans. Despite their fragility, they could get used to anything.

She kept her eyes peeled for a man in a red hat. That's how the agency had told them to identify each other- a red hat and a red dress.

She felt him before she saw him, which meant he was looking at her intently, and setting off her hunter's senses. He was close, but she didn't whip around to look in his direction. Instead, she sat back against the bench coolly, and looked up into the beautiful blue sky, which was fading to purple before it finally turned to night. She waited until he was close enough to hear her and then she said with a grin, "Not very sneaky. I could feel you the whole way."

A voice responded, "I wanted you to feel me. I couldn't take my eyes off of you."

The sound of his voice took Melanie's breath away. It was luxurious, with the hint of an accent she couldn't place. It was the most sultry and aristocratic sound she'd ever heard in her whole life, with just the tiniest hint of a growl lurking under the surface. This was a voice that sounded as if it could belong to a lion. The King of the Beasts, but still a beast at heart.

She whipped around toward the voice as if it magnetized her. She couldn't see him yet.

Then suddenly, she felt the warmth of a body next to hers, behind where she'd been looking. She felt the prickling awareness of his large body behind her, and she reveled in his attention and the fear of her vulnerable backside facing a strong male.

After taking a deep breath, she turned to him. She said, "You still managed to sneak up on me."

He smiled at her. With a casual wave of the hand, he said, "I wanted to give you a chance for love at first sight. For that, we need the element of surprise."

Melanie let him see her checking him out. He was lean, with sinewy muscle and deliciously long, straight lines all over his body. Long legs, long torso, a strong line for his chin.

He wore pointed leather shoes, European imports, expensive. Melanie could smell that the leather was authentic and new. He had on dark blue jeans, boot cut, but pressed and tailored to fit him perfectly. The thin red sweater he wore looked as if it strained against the muscles of his chest and biceps. It was tucked perfectly into his jeans.

He was so well put-together that the very polished nature of his outfit demanded you tear every piece of clothing off him, after you'd stared at him and salivated. She nodded appreciatively and looked at his face.

The first thing she noticed was the intense gray eyes. They flashed silver like the moon, and burned with the intensity most shifters could only manage when they were in the midst of changing into full wolf. They were perfect orbs and he was sending them all over her body. She felt their heat wherever they lit. She wished she'd worn a lighter jacket, something more revealing. She was far from feeling silly about showing off now.

His hair was styled like a classic movie star, with only one misbehaving front lock breaking ranks and dancing cheekily on his broad forehead. He looked like a Golden Age movie star, and he was clearly playing up the comparison. He even had the thin lines of a pencil mustache. His dark-black hair looked soft to the touch. His lips looked yummy and perfectly pouted. His cheekbones looked as if they could cut better than a knife.

"Who are you supposed to be, Clark Gable?" she quipped with a grin

"I feel more of an affinity to Errol Flynn," he said with a slow roll of that deliriously sexy, but hard to place accent. "But I won't dispute a similarity with Mr. Gable."

His magnetism was incredible. She deeply regretted not inviting him straight to the house. The Paranormal True Mate Dating Agency made it clear they wanted you to "sample" the wolf they sent and discover if you were sexually compatible quickly.

She sure as hell wanted to discover a few things about Errol Flynn here. Starting with the feel of kissing his washboard abs, promptly followed by biting a chunk of that juicy strong thigh.

"Shall we take a walk?" he asked.

She joined him on a winding path that cut leisurely through the park.

He admitted without the slightest trace of apology, "I am afraid the Agency gave me your name and particulars, but I believe they didn't give you the same advantage? I hate having a rigged game."

She laughed. "So you think you know me? From an online dating profile?"

He shook his head. "I know enough to know something you don't. Or rather, to tell you something you already know, but won't admit."

"There's a lot about me I wouldn't admit to a stranger," she said, trying to be enigmatic.

He spoke very quietly, so she had to lean in to hear him, which she wondered if he did on purpose to get her to walk even closer to him, "You deserve more from this life than you're getting."

She took a step away. She said, "Heh. So do most women."

He nodded, as if he agreed completely. Then he said, "So if you know that already, why don't you ask for more?"

She didn't really have an answer. She'd always seen herself as a strong, principled woman who demanded what she wanted from life and the people around her. But somehow, all the things she asked for were for the benefit of other people and not herself.

After thinking for a while as they strolled, she said, "Alright, give me more, then. Starting with your name, and a fun fact about you."

He glanced at her with a wry smile. "A fun fact?"

She smiled. "Yeah. Something so I know you're a real person with a real past."

He thought for a brief moment, and then said, "My name is Jean. I'm not from the US."

Melanie shook her head. "No way, that won't cut it. So your name is basically John, and you're foreign. That counts you among, oh, I don't know, a billion guys in the world. No, tell me something about *you*, in particular."

He gestured toward her. "You're kind of trying to ruin my whole mystique. I like to cultivate mystery. It makes . . . things . . . more exciting." When he said "things," he caught her eyes and then his gaze roved over her body.

It gave her a thrilling feeling that ran from her toes up to her neck, all of which wanted to be licked by him. But she couldn't let her animal instincts take over, quite yet. She wanted to know something real about him first.

"I think you'll retain your air of mystery just fine," she said. "Here, I'll give you an example, about me." She had one locked and loaded. "I was a cheerleader in high school, until I got kicked out for clocking another girl in the eye."

He grinned wildly, heartily entertained by the story implicit in that shared little fact. He said, "Ah, I see now. You want me to embarrass myself."

She said, "Hey, I'm not embarrassed. She deserved it."

He said, "I have a hard time seeing you as a cheerleader. But then again, in a way, it fits. You are not the type to sit quietly."

She shrugged. "Hiding in plain sight. Being . . . like us . . . in an American high school. Better to participate than to try to stay in the corner. Kids notice the wallflowers a lot more than they notice the kids who fit in." She stopped talking and jabbed a finger toward Jean. "Your turn."

He pondered. She enjoyed the classic look of his masculine profile. Finally he put up his index finger and brightened with a smile, as if he'd come up with an invention, or a big discovery for the universe.

He said, "When I was a child, I played Peter Pan. I always liked that story," he said quietly, "I would've liked the ability to fly." Then he caught her eye and laughed at himself a little. "But I am not alone in that, many people like the story."

She said, "That is a great fun fact. Well done."

They'd stopped walking. She stood only a few feet in front of him, facing his gorgeously sculpted face, underneath the dark cover of a swaying tree. She glanced around and realized they were alone in a clearing.

"You seem to have lured me somewhere we're all by our lonesome," she said, trying to sound playful, but loading her phrase with a husky longing she couldn't hide,

He stepped forward and closed the distance between them. He gripped her chin and tipped her mouth up so it would easily meet his.

He whispered, "We are alone, but not lonesome."

Then he pressed his luscious lips to her waiting, wishful mouth. As he kissed her, he pressed his body into hers with insistent warmth that made her feel comfortable at first and then unbearably warm. She wanted to tear off her clothes and feel that burn all over.

He said, "Take what you deserve, Melanie."

She purred, "I will."

MELANIE

Her first move, as he pressed his lean, strong body against hers in a way that couldn't be denied, was to reach down and grip his crotch. She wanted to feel the warmest part of his body; the most sensitive. He moaned and moved back a bit in surprise, but then he adjusted himself so she could get a better grip.

He slid his hands underneath her coat and, in an effortless move that she did not even attempt to fight, he threw off her bulky coat. Keeping one hand on his burning hot crotch, she slid her hand up to pull his sweater out of his jeans. She ran her hand over his impressive abs, which were just as hard and unrelenting to the touch as she had imagined.

He gripped the back of her thighs and slid his hands up under her dress, hooking his thumbs through her lacy panties. With a swift move and a roar that thrilled her, he tore the flimsy fabric in half. She squealed as his huge hands gripped her bare ass and pulled her up. She wrapped her legs around his hips, tearing his sweater off over his head with reckless abandon. She threw it off, not worrying about where it landed or recovering it later. All she could think about was how badly she wanted them both to be naked together, in the woods, rutting like wolves were meant to do.

He pushed her body viciously against the trunk of the tree and dove his face into her neck. She squealed and giggled in a way she hadn't in decades. He kissed her collarbone and licked down to her dress's neckline.

With an irritated snarl at the fabric blocking his tongue from exploring her cleavage and her breasts, he pulled the dress off of her in a single movement, like a magician taking off a tablecloth and magically leaving the rest of the food on it. He was utterly graceful.

She scrabbled at his fly, desperate to get it open and release his cock. She was having a difficult time. Her lust and desire were causing her to shake violently, and every time his tongue flickered over her breasts and inched ever closer to her nipples, her whole body convulsed and she yelled.

He took her little mouth in his wide, wet one, and then whispered to her, "We must be quieter, or we will be caught."

She said, "I don't give a damn." He grinned widely and flicked up his huge, warm thumbs to flicker over her nipples. She squirmed underneath his touch and whimpered.

She wasn't screaming anymore. She was begging, "Please, please," repeating over and over as he teased her nipples.

Finally, he stopped flickering over them and enjoying her desperate pleading. He put his thumbs straight onto her nipples and caressed them. She said, "Yes," in a pleading moan directly into his ear, and he moaned back in sympathetic pleasure.

Unable to take any more, she gripped him by the hair viciously and said, "Take me. Now."

He said wryly, "As you order, madam."

Keeping her legs wrapped around his torso, he finished unzipping, and dropped his jeans and underwear. He stepped out of them quickly and kicked them out of the way so they wouldn't distract him.

She opened her legs with joy, driven crazy by lust, as he looked down to her wet, open vagina. She waited for him to slide inside her, but their idyllic outdoor lovemaking was interrupted by the annoying, all-too-modern sound of her phone ringing.

She sighed so hard it was really a growl. She held up a finger and said, "One second, I have to check who it is."

A little surprised she was letting herself get distracted, he dropped her legs as requested. Suddenly cognizant of her own nakedness, she stooped quickly to where her coat had been discarded and pulled her phone out of the pocket. She checked the caller ID irritably, annoyed that someone dared to interrupt the first fun she'd had in a decade.

It was Carl's number. She really did growl this time; angry, heartbroken and scared. She pressed the phone to answer.

She yelled, "And just where in the hell have you been?"

The voice that came back over the line was not familiar. It sounded like a creaking door hinge in an old building that should have been condemned; ancient and inordinately spooky.

It said, "I'm here with your husband, Madame. Now, what you'll want to know is . . . Where is that?"

Her throat clenched and her bile rose. For all of her grief over Carl's abandoning her, she loved him. Hell, that's the only reason she gave a damn that he was still gone.

She yelled into the phone, "Who the hell are you? Why do you have Carl's phone?"

The ancient voice responded, "At the risk of sounding clichéd, I have Carl's phone because he's a bit indisposed right now. To be frank, your husband owes me a rather large debt. He informed us that you would be able to pay said debt."

Melanie couldn't stop shouting. "A debt? What debt?"

The ancient voice sighed, as if it felt oh-so-very sorry for the foolish deeds of the children that surrounded it. Then it explained, "Your husband has an unfortunate gambling problem. He's run into a losing streak as of late. As of now, his debts to us run to about $800,000."

Melanie was shocked into spitting out the truth. "We don't have that kind of money."

The ancient voice sounded surprised. "Oh? He seemed to think you could pay it. I guess we'll have to go with option two. Or three."

Melanie roared into the phone, "Listen, I don't know who the fuck you think you are, but you must not know who the fuck I am. Because I am going to find you, and I am going to tear out your fucking eyeballs and feed them to you."

Jean had been listening carefully, concerned at Melanie's obvious anguish, and he winced at her threat. "Remind me not to piss you off," he said sincerely.

The ancient voice was nonplussed. It said slowly, again as if it was speaking to a child, "Your threats are meaningless to me. You can either pay the $800,000, bring us your firstborn child, or we kill your husband. Even if we kill him, you'll still owe us, regardless. We don't forgive debts with blood. His death will be but a warning."

Melanie waved her hand around as if she was trying to clear fog away from her vision. She said, "Wait, what the hell did you say? Bring you our firstborn?"

The ancient voice said, "Your husband had to put up some kind of collateral. We knew we couldn't trust him to pay us back. So, he offered your son. I believe his name is Michael? Such a young, strong wolf. I believe he will make a fantastic serving minion."

Melanie was so overcome with confusion and rage that she whispered, "What?" and almost dropped the phone.

She recovered in time to hear the ancient voice telling her, "We really treat our servants well. Especially the werewolf minions. He'll live in absolute comfort as our pet and errand boy. It's a swell gig, as they say. Your kind can't expect much better. You're not good for cerebral work. But you are fun to fondle and play with."

Melanie's throat squeezed shut entirely. She pushed her voice out in a rasping croak, "Where are you?"

The ancient voice ignored her question. "You have three days to collect the money and call me at this number. This is me being generous. I hope you'll be grateful. Once you have the money ready, I will provide further instructions. Remember: if you don't call me in seventy-two hours – not a minute more – we will kill Carl. And you'll still owe us the money or your first born. So long."

Melanie heard the phone hang up but she couldn't move. She stood locked in the stillness of the forest, as if she could come up with the right thing to say to erase all the horrible words from that horrible voice.

As she stood in the weighted silence, Jean finally ventured to speak gently. "Melanie," he murmured, "What has happened?"

She did her best to explain, but saying it aloud made it real, and her hot, rage-filled tears fell. Strange, it had been such a long time since she'd cried. She'd forgotten how uncomfortable it truly was.

When she reached the end of her sad, garbled tale of woe, Jean said, "May I be so bold as to say I hate your husband?"

She nodded. "Yes, you may. But I love him, damn it, and even if I didn't, we have a pup. A wonderful, miraculous pup who loves his father so much, even though that father has tried to sell him—" With that, she was no longer able to speak coherently. She fell into Jean's waiting arms and sobbed.

He rocked her gently, whispering soothing things in her ear in a language she didn't know.

Once her crying calmed down, he kept his grip on her but stepped back to look her in the eye. He said, "Melanie. I have only just met you. But I can tell you are a woman of grand feeling, and a wonderful mother. Even if you were a shitty mother, you would not deserve this. I will help you, if you wish."

The melodious tones of his magically gorgeous voice soothed her enough for her brain to start working again. She said, "Okay, okay," breathing deeply. Finally, she said, "No one is taking my son. But we have no idea who this person is, or why they're so confident. That scares me."

Jean nodded, but did not speak, respectfully waiting for her to continue her train of thought.

Melanie took a deep breath and wiped her eyes. She looked into Jean's to see if she could find a trace of fear and found none. That didn't surprise her.

He was a werewolf, and he hadn't heard the horrible voice on the phone. Melanie wasn't one to scare easy, either. But something about the confidence and . . . nonchalance in the voice had horrified her. Melanie's brain was sputtering back into action. She remembered her pack had experience with kidnapping. They'd recovered Davie last year, when he was stolen by other werewolves.

Whoever had been on the phone wasn't a werewolf, Melanie was sure. But she'd learned a long time ago to rely on the pack in bad situations. Several wolves were better than one.

She sighed and wiped her face on her sleeve, not giving a damn about her smeared makeup. She said to Jean, "Ready to meet my family?"

A smile flickered at the corner of his mouth, but he must have recognized she was not quite ready for levity. So he just nodded and, once they'd recovered the clothes that they hadn't torn irreparably, he followed her out of the woods toward her car.

DANVER

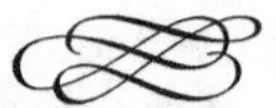

The pack was gathered around the dining table in various positions of incredulity, rage, and fear. Melanie had allowed her son, Michael, to join the conversation. He had already had his maturation ceremony, after all. By werewolf standards, he was a man. But he still glared at his mom's "friend" Jean like a child who hated strangers.

Danver supposed he was being hypocritical for judging the boy. He was glaring at Jean quite a bit, as well. He didn't like his mustache. Jean looked like a man who was trying too hard to be charming. It was Danver's experience that the people who looked the most charming were the most snakelike inside. But it seemed that the man had offered Melanie his help, thus far with no immediately noticeable ulterior motive. It was a dangerous thing to get involved in, just for the chance of some sex, so Danver was willing to let the man into their home and to offer his help. But that didn't mean he trusted him. At all.

Melanie went over the details of the phone call, and although they all had a million questions, they waited for her to finish sharing everything she knew, before they responded. When she wrapped up by carefully saying, "They threatened to take Michael, too, if the debts weren't paid," Danver got the feeling she was hiding something in the way she said it. But he let it go.

Cassidy and Wes responded at the same time, a funny habit of theirs that came from neither of them really listening to the other.

Cassidy reached out for Melanie's hand and said, "I'm so sorry, Mel." She was such a softhearted human. Melanie appreciated the support and squeezed her hand in return.

Wes sat up in his chair and yelled, "I'm going to kill Carl. If they don't kill him, then I'm going to kill him."

Cassidy shot him a look and mouthed, "Shut up,"

But he said, "What? He's put the whole pack in danger. Hell, forget about us, I know he doesn't like you and me, Cassidy, but he put his mate and pup in the cross hairs of whatever weirdos these people are. How do you lose $800,000 gambling and not realize you have a problem?"

Jean chimed in, "You're assuming 'people'. They might not be people." Everyone looked at him.

Danver hated the casual way he was leaning against the counter. He looked as if he belonged there. Danver still felt out of place, and he'd been there for a year.

However, because he wasn't the type to ignore a guest totally, even if he didn't like him, Danver asked him, "What do you mean?"

"It is my understanding that by 'people' we usually mean, 'the living.' But hearing Melanie's description of the voice . . . That it had the quality of the undead," Jean said, his voice the vocal embodiment of a shrug, no matter the import of what he was saying.

"You mean like a zombie?" Melanie asked with a note of derisive disbelief that Danver appreciated.

Wes said seriously, which was weird for him, because he never said anything seriously, "You mean a vampire."

Jean pointed at Wes and said, "As they say, bingo."

Melanie looked between the two of them, and Danver could read her mind, because he was feeling exactly the same way.

At the same time, the two of them said, "Vampires aren't real."

Danver continued, "At least, they haven't been for two hundred years. They were wiped out after the wolves in Europe signed the Final Concord."

It was a kind of horrific agreement; some of the older werewolves still remembered hearing of it. The werewolves who made it were all ancient alpha wolves among the European clans. It was a contract, where they agreed to band together to hunt down the vampires, who were in danger of revealing the existence of the supernatural to the humans.

The subterfuge and slaughter that followed were not things the werewolves liked to talk about. In fact, it was bad taste to bring it up at all. So why the hell was Jean talking about it?

Wes said, "When I was on my own and traveling, I heard about . . . some cabals. Or hives. Or whatever the hell vampires call their groups, in the northwest. If you hang around unsavory characters in Seattle, you'll hear about them."

His mate and his sister glared at him viciously. He put up his hands in a submissive gesture, protesting, "Hey, we established that I used to be a shady asshole a long time ago. Now I have a baby. I'm significantly less shady now. But when I was very, very shady . . . well, you talk to bad people, and you hear bad things. None of which I was directly involved with."

The women didn't look super-satisfied with this explanation, but they stopped glaring.

Danver said, "So there are vampires in Washington. And they have Carl, and they've threatened Michael." He sighed. This was messier than anything the family had gotten into before.

"How are you so sure that it's vampires, who have Carl?" Melanie asked with a note of exasperation and confusion,

Wes quipped, "Yeah, maybe he's a run-of-the-mill moron and got mixed up with the human mob?"

Melanie glared at him, so Jean cut in by saying, "Your mate; he is a werewolf, correct?" Melanie said he was.

Wes said, "By some standards, he can be considered a werewolf." Melanie turned and growled at him, and he continued, "I've seen the guy outrun by rabbits."

Jean hid any trace of superiority concerning Melanie's unimpressive husband, which Danver considered the first positive in his favor. At least it didn't seem as if the guy wanted to supplant Melanie's rightful mate; not by subterfuge, anyway.

Jean clarified, "But he could definitely overpower a human, correct? And he cannot be killed by regular human means? So it is unlikely that humans have captured and kept him."

Nobody could argue with that.

Cassidy, the only human, couldn't help but admit, "Vampires? I thought you guys existing was crazy enough. I don't need to hear that Dracula is real, too."

"Very real." Melanie said with a frown, "and very scary, if our grandparents' stories are to be believed about the concord."

Jean pointed out, "There is at least one bright side." They all waited, and he said, "At least we know it is possible for a werewolf to defeat a vampire."

Melanie said with a tone of defeat, "Werewolves plural. Whole clans. We don't even know for sure that's who we're after. We have no clues."

Danver stepped forward. "You've got a pack. We'll do anything to keep your family safe." Once he saw she looked at least a little comforted by that fact, if not much, he continued, "Wes, you said you heard about these vampires when you were in Seattle? It sounds as if they were into illegal loans and that kind of thing?"

Wes said, "Hey, I'm no expert, and I won't say every vampire in Washington is into it, but I heard about several scary groups that were definitely run by vamps."

Danver nodded. "If you heard about them in person, you can learn more about them on the internet." He looked at Melanie. "We'll find them. Or at least, we'll get close enough that maybe we can get some leverage, so we don't go in blind, when you speak to them next."

She was normally such a stoic, put-together woman, but right now, he could tell, by the way she held Cassidy's hand, that she was scared. She was gripping it so hard Cassidy winced a bit.

Wes stood up and put his hands on his sister's shoulders. It was nice to see. Usually, the extent of their interaction was sarcastic remarks and playful (or not so playful) smacks. The pack didn't have an Alpha, and thus far that hadn't been a problem. It was a small enough group, with clear enough responsibilities that no big arguments had arisen, which needed an ultimate decider. Wes didn't seem eager for the role, but it felt good to Danver to see him maturing and taking care of his mate and his sister, better and better every day.

Danver didn't know how long he could continue ignoring his feelings for Melanie. After this debacle, if they recovered Carl alive . . . he wasn't sure he'd be able to stand being around the guy.

Maybe after this final task, it would really be time for him to leave. He'd always felt like an interloper. Being the one unmated, adult male was rough.

After comforting his sister for a moment, Wes looked at Danver and said, "So we start the research now and we'll leave for Seattle in the morning?"

They both looked at Wes and said, "We?", again in sync – an awkward habit that Danver and Melanie had picked up recently.

Melanie said, "Who the hell said you're going anywhere? It's my mate that's fucked up. You have a baby to take care of."

Wes said, "Yeah, well, me and Danver are like the dynamic duo, alright? I can't let my buddy go into battle without me."

Danver didn't say anything. He didn't think Wes's true reason for wanting them to be the ones who went, was protecting him. Melanie figured it out, too.

"I don't care about your macho bullshit." she snarled at Wes. "If anybody is going to go save Carl, it's me. I won't accept your help, either. You have a mate and a baby to worry about. And someone needs to stay to help Michael."

Michael shot up, absolutely livid in that all-consuming way that only teenagers can do. He was so angry his teeth were elongating and his hands were gnarling up, as if he was going to burst into the change right there.

"I don't need anyone's protection!" he screamed. "I hate all of you! I'm going with you to go get Dad!"

Melanie slammed her fist on the table and snarled. "Sit down, Michael. I said 'help', not protect. You need to stay here and protect Davie. You need to help the pack. That's what a man does. Your father forgot that."

Michael calmed down, when he realized he wasn't being treated like a baby. At least, that's how his mother was spinning it. From his shaking hands, Danver could tell he was glad to have an excuse to back down and stay at home, away from vampires and his father's shame.

Danver wondered how it would have felt to be called to rescue his own father. His father had been such a powerful wolf. At least, it had seemed that way to Danver when he was young. He decided it would have been distorted and confusing, going to rescue someone whom he looked up to so much. He felt sorry for Michael. He must be struggling with this information, more than anyone else in the pack.

"Whoever these people are, they were strong enough to overpower and imprison Carl," Melanie said firmly, "And they could probably find out where I live. That means the whole pack is in danger." She looked for at both Wes and Michael, who looked equally chastised, a very long time. Then she said, "What's the first law of pack safety?"

With a frown, Michael repeated what he'd been taught, "You never leave the cave unguarded. Especially if there are pups."

"There's nothing more important than the home and the babies." Melanie said with finality. " I will go to Seattle. Jean has agreed to help me. Wes, you have to stay here. Cassidy, I'm glad to hear you're not foolish enough to offer to go."

Cassidy shook her head vigorously. "I've fought werewolves and poachers before. I'm a steady shot. But I don't have any guns with special wooden stakes that'll kill a vampire. Not that I know of, anyway."

Melanie pointed at her son, trying to maintain eye contact even though he wouldn't look at her, "You stay here. You protect the pack. You guard the pup. You got it?"

He didn't respond. She snarled. He yelled, "Yes, God, I got it."

It looked so much like human interactions with their sulking teenagers that Danver almost smiled. Guess some things were standard across species.

Everyone looked resigned to their lot in life. Melanie hadn't ordered Danver to stay or go. She was waiting for him to make a choice.

Danver said, "So we'll do some research tonight, and then Melanie and I will head to Seattle in the morning."

"You, the lovely Melanie, and the dashing Jean, who has so kindly offered to help total strangers battle vampires." Jean said with a bright, happy tone.

Wes narrowed his eyes at Jean. Danver had never liked Wes more than at that particular moment. "Why are you so willing to risk life and limb to help us?" Wes asked.

Jean smiled with bright, white, perfectly arranged teeth. "Because it is what I do. I am a vampire hunter."

Wes threw his arms up and said, "How convenient!"

Jean quipped, "Not for the vampire kidnappers. It will be very inconvenient for them."

Danver suddenly had a lot more questions about this Jean guy than answers. But he didn't want to waste time asking them. If they were really going up against a vampire hive, they'd need all the help they could get.

DANVER

It was 5 AM. The pups and the human were asleep. Before she'd given up for the night, Cassidy had suggested someone go through Carl's desktop for clues. Danver had been given the dubious honor of rooting through Carl's browser history and saved files. Melanie didn't want to do it and, given how many secrets Carl had been keeping, Danver didn't want to put her through it.

Wes said, "I already hate the guy, even more so now he's brought this shit down on my sister. I don't need more reasons to want to kill him."

Danver didn't argue with him, but he certainly wondered if he wanted to have more reasons to hate Melanie's mate. It was hard enough not to grab her and give her the pleasure he doubted she'd felt in years.

The smug look on Jean's face made him wonder how far they'd gotten in their date, before Melanie had received the call. Danver tried to shove the thought from his head, but it kept sneaking back in. Instead, he focused on the files in front of him. He'd worked in IT for a little bit, in between being an actuary and his current job as a ranch hand, so it wasn't hard for him to bypass Carl's password and get into the system. He worried briefly that Carl had stronger protection protocols, but it became clear he was a gamer, not a tech nerd.

His browsing history was pretty innocuous, for the most part. Just gamer sites. Not even any porn sites (that Danver's limited knowledge of them could tell), but he guessed he'd probably deleted that history. There were ways to pull it up, but Danver wanted to see if he could find anything relevant, before he really dug in. Everything seemed to be fairly benign Google searches or gamer sites, however.

Danver clicked on a few of the sites and started exploring their content, wondering how the hell Carl had managed to hide a hundreds-of-thousands gambling habit away from everyone. After he entered a site called "esportchampionshiphuddle.net," it all became clear. Carl had entered this site for the first time, about a year ago. After visiting it occasionally, for five or so weeks after that, he'd been on it almost every day for every month following. It was a video game sports betting site.

It kind of blew Danver's mind. You weren't even watching real people play all the time. Some of the games on the site were computers playing other computers, and people were still betting truckloads of money. The pots were huge. Some of the games were in the millions. Which meant it would be easy enough to lose the amount Danver had lost.

But where the heck did he get it from? He decided to look at Carl's messages now, to see whether anything was in there that would clue him in. He pulled up the app that let Carl read his messages from the computer. He scrolled through the chats looking for any name he didn't recognize.

He found the girl Carl had been messaging, the one that Melanie had called "someone else in Seattle." The one he was cheating on Melanie with.

Danver didn't want to dig into this particular depravity. He couldn't imagine what a man, who had Melanie, would still feel the need to look for. But there was the thinnest chance she was a clue.

Pretty quickly, he got a sense of what Carl was looking for that he couldn't get from Melanie. The woman he was texting, named Lara, was very sexual and very submissive. Anything Carl asked for, she'd agree to, or take a picture. There were plenty of pictures scattered throughout their chats. No wonder Melanie had instantly understood what was happening. It took only a glance to see this conversation was NC-17. Carl definitely encouraged it, even going so far as to send his own pictures.

Danver certainly hadn't needed to see that. He tried to skim quickly, focusing on the text, for information about whom Carl hung out with when he was in Seattle. Then, one picture of Lara made him stop in his tracks. It wasn't even one of the filthier pictures. She was cupping her bare breasts in both hands, which made Danver wonder who was holding the camera.

Judging from the tattoo on her shoulder, he had a guess. Over the course of the evening, Jean had given them some background on vampires. One of the subjects he'd gone into in detail is the vampire's "thralls," or humans who swore loyalty in exchange for the promise of everlasting life or other favors.

Thralls always had a tattoo of their master, except it wasn't just a tattoo. It was a brand, the same as the ranch did to their cattle. The ranch's brand was a "W" inside a heart, because Cassidy had originally opened the ranch to double as a wolf rescue, for the Mexican Wolf population in New Mexico. Ironically, the W for Wolf had a double meaning in her life now.

This brand on Lara was disturbing. The brand's background was the shape of a pig, and on top of that, there was an added layer of a tattooing. It added blood to the pig, as if it was bleeding out.

Danver considered screenshotting it and texting it to himself from the computer, but then he realized that was stupid. The vampires had Carl's phone. They'd see if he sent anything to anyone, and Danver didn't want to let on that they knew vampires were holding him.

So he left it up on the screen and rushed downstairs. Everyone looked up when he entered, except Melanie. He imagined she didn't exactly relish hearing whatever news he was going to bring.

Instead of revealing what he'd found to everyone, he locked eyes with Jean. "Come on, vampire hunter," he said, waving for him to follow him upstairs. Jean followed with the barest hint of a smile. Once they got upstairs, he asked, "Are you going to scold me? Or have I not been the baddest boy in the house?"

Danver sneered. He didn't like this guy's flippant attitude.

He gestured to the study where Carl kept his gaming computers, including the desktop Danver had been accessing. Jean walked in and toward the one lit screen.

His eyebrows popped up and his lips pursed, a very European expression of surprise. Danver wondered, again, where the hell this guy had come from.

Jean shook his head and clucked his tongue. He said, "It looks as if Carl has not so much been a bad boy, as fallen in with a very bad girl."

Danver ignored his playful wording, which he found ridiculous and unnecessary. He confirmed, "So you recognize the brand?"

Jean nodded slowly. His smile disappeared from his face, and he suddenly looked much older and the mustache looked even sillier, to Danver's eyes.

"Yes. I recognize it," he said with some hesitation, as if he didn't want to mention even this small bit of information if it wasn't necessary. "It's Buld. An Ancient One. A survivor of our species' fabled concord. He is a survivor of many things."

He looked at it again, more closely, and then amended his statement. "At least, it's in Buld's hive. Under his control. Normally Buld's brand is a stuck boar, done in this style. But I've seen this pig variation in younger vampires who've sworn him fealty."

Danver nodded. "At least it's not Buld himself, then. We'll be dealing with someone younger, and hopefully weaker?"

Jean laughed. "Young and weak are not the qualities of a vampire. They hide their new, uh, shall we say converts, for at least a hundred years. So any vampire is at least one hundred years old, and, then, however old they were as humans."

Danver narrowed his eyes and stared at Jean with an intensity that could turn into a battle between two werewolf males. He asked quietly, "How did you become a vampire hunter?"

Jean's face turned into a nasty snarl, but a laugh still came out of his maw. He said, "I would like to tell you it was merely for sport, my friend, or a misplaced sense of adventure. But those who hunt vampires for fun, well, they die, because there is no fun to be had there."

Danver waited for his true answer. After a deep, calming breath, Jean said "I have no family. I will not give you more, because I do not owe you more. But I will tell you that much."

After a moment of silence, while Danver weighed up whether he believed a man who relied so much on his charm and his quick words. Then, he noticed that genuine grief was weighing down the man's face. Danver nodded and leaned forward to shut down the computer.

Brightening up and shaking himself off, Jean said, "I believe I know where we may start to find this vassal of Buld's. Great work. It must have taken you quite a bit of . . . reading . . . to find that particular picture."

Jean gestured to the bare breasts still on the screen, and the message below it. Lara asked Carl, "What do you want to do to my breasts, Daddy Wolf?"

Danver shook his head. "The fool. He revealed he was a werewolf. To this random human."

Jean sighed and shrugged his shoulders dramatically. "We men are fools for what is beautiful. We may judge this man, if we return alive from this favor we do for a mated woman, who does not belong to us."

Danver blinked at Jean, who merely gave him a knowing look, and walked away. After a second of confusion and embarrassment, Danver followed.

Maybe Jean was right. He was risking life and limb for a woman who could never love him as a mate. But he was in too deep to turn back.

He couldn't turn his back on Melanie. Not until he knew she was safe. And even then, . . . he didn't know how he'd find the strength to leave her at last.

MELANIE

After a year away from Seattle, Melanie found the gray skies much more depressing than she remembered. She'd been paranoid the whole way up, too, wondering if the vampires had spies in the airport. They'd all decided flying was worth the saved time, even though it was more of a security risk. Now they were in a hotel, under fake names, after getting weird looks from the front desk staff. Melanie had smirked at the girl handing her the key, saying, "What, you don't get a lot of women traveling with two extremely hot men?"

The girl looked embarrassed to be staring, but that didn't stop her from continuing to stare as Jean and Danver brought the bags into the room with ease. Melanie stared too. From their beautiful faces to their sweetly shaped asses, they were delectable men.

It was like traveling with guys who played superheroes. Or porn stars. Melanie wondered how she was going to deal with both of them in the same room as her every night.

She had some pretty good ideas of how she'd like to "deal" with it. She was under a lot of stress, and all that tension and fear needed a good release.

It was their second night in Seattle. That meant tomorrow would

43

be the end of the three days the vampire had promised on the phone. Then they'd be looking for that $800,000 she didn't have.

Melanie, Danver, and Jean had done some good reconnaissance, since they'd been in town. Jean and Danver seemed to agree they'd narrowed down the location of at least one of the vampire gang's hideaways. They planned to scope it out the next day, while Melanie kept the guy busy on the phone, whenever he called. She wasn't looking forward to it. She hated the memory of that voice so much. She couldn't help but hate her mate every time she thought about it.

Melanie held her bag of toiletries in her hand, but the thought of the massive amount of money her husband had gambled away made her lose her shit. She turned and chucked her bag across the room. It slammed into the wall and flopped to the floor.

There was a crack in the hotel's plaster now. She growled, annoyed with herself for not keeping herself under control, and annoyed at Carl for dragging them into this situation.

Jean looked at the hole in the wall with widened eyes. He grabbed the toiletry bag and held it out to Melanie. "Madame, I believe you have dropped this?"

Danver grunted, "And now we've lost our security deposit."

Melanie took the bag and went to put it in the bathroom. "I know that was stupid. But you know what else is stupid? Losing $800,000 on video games. E-sports. What a fucking joke. God, that's enough for a house."

At the thought of her husband plunking down enough for a home on his own pleasure instead of spending it on his family's welfare – even promising his own son as collateral – she broke into tears. She hadn't realized her tears were being storing up so aggressively, but now they were out.

She started apologizing for the outburst, but Danver was at her side in a second. He sat down beside her and held her, telling her, "You have nothing to be sorry for."

She leaned into his shoulder and let the tears fall. It was soothing to let it out finally. Especially with his warm, strong arms wrapped around her.

She heard Jean's smooth voice offering, "Would a massage help?"

Danver glared at him, and Jean quickly said, "Only a friendly massage. Unless Melanie would like a happy ending."

Melanie laughed and said, "That sounds relaxing and nice, actually."

Danver grunted but he didn't protest. He also didn't move from Melanie's side as Jean slid in behind her. Jean moved his legs around her and wrapped them so she was trapped by his massive thighs and calves.

She squealed and Danver said, "Friendly, huh?"

Jean said, "What? This? It is only for leverage. Better massage this way."

He began to rub Melanie's shoulders. Danver didn't move from her side. Melanie, feeling impulsive and desirous of his touch, too, reached out and grabbed his hand to hold.

To her surprise, he didn't remove it. He wouldn't look at her, but he locked her fingers up in his and looked down at the ground.

Jean murmured, "This is much more difficult to do well with your shirt on, Madame. And that bra. It's simply in the way."

Danver growled by way of an answer.

Jean protested, "I only want her to have the best possible massage. Please, I am a professional. This is but a disinterested recommendation. To improve her experience."

"Improve my experience, huh?" Melanie said with a smirk. "I'd sure like to have a good experience at some point. Off with the shirt, then."

Jean pushed his luck. "And the pesky bra?"

Melanie looked at Danver. She said, "I don't want to make you uncomfortable."

He looked supremely uncomfortable. As if he would rather be anywhere in the world, but this spot, right now, but he couldn't move because he'd been turned to stone.

Finally, he grunted, "Do whatever you want." He took his hand away from hers and grabbed the television remote. He turned on some movie, ignoring Melanie's pained expression.

She wanted his hand back in hers. She wanted him touching her, so badly. Why did he have to be so difficult and pout about everything?

She said, "Fine. If I'm going to do whatever I want, I want to have an incredible massage. Off with the bra."

She stripped. She looked at him over her shoulder and caught him looking. But he whipped his eyes off her and tried to keep them glued to the television screen.

Jean really wasn't kidding about being a professional. His hands felt like butter, except when they needed to be hard and firm on the trouble spots in her back. She felt as if she was melting underneath him.

She didn't care if she was moaning or whimpering with pleasure. She deserved to relax, even if Danver wanted to be a spoilsport.

When Jean moved to her lower back, the feelings changed from simple comfort and relaxation to deep-seated pleasure. It was as if his hands had touched a nerve that shot from his gentle, firm pressure on her back to her clitoris. A deep burn started up in her groin and warmed her whole lower body. Her breath shot in with a sharp intake. She was shocked to have such an immediate, sexual response to such a simple touch.

At the sound of her surprised breath and then the deepening, lustful breathing that followed, Jean let loose a small purr of satisfaction. Melanie also felt Danver's attention on her. That was the most thrilling thing, and she felt as if she couldn't hold back from the pleasure that promised her.

She arched her back and ground her hips into the bed. She felt all of her animal instincts driving her to thrust her hips and grind her clit against everything, preferably one of the incredibly sexy men in her room.

She felt as if she was going absolutely wild. It was a feeling that she'd only felt before on hunts, and even then, she hadn't felt that thrill in a long time. The feeling of utterly being as you were meant to be.

Feeling Jean's hands on her lower back and Danver's attention focused on her so absolutely, she felt like a goddess and the basest creature, all wrapped into one. She let her heavy breathing turn into moaning, especially as Jean dove his hands beneath the lines of her pants and started stroking her hips and her ass.

As her animal moans turned to mortal begging, she whimpered, "Touch me." She didn't say, "Touch me, Jean," because she wanted Danver, too. Jean responded by sliding his strong, gentle hands into the front of her pants and underneath her panties. The memory of how he'd torn them off during their first encounter drove her crazy. She shifted her hips so it was easier for him to rub her clit.

He started exploring all around. Except it was too expert and focused to call it "exploring." It was more like hunting.

Yes, he was hunting the perfect spots for her pleasure. He was encircling her clit and sensing along her labia, testing what made her jump. When she jumped, squirmed or squealed, he pursued that spot with a rabid focus until he could find an even bigger quarry to hunt down.

She was in his lap now, utterly at the mercy of his expert hands. With one hand, he gripped her breasts, viciously taking pleasure from squeezing them tightly, while with the other, he turned her whole sense of self and all of her awareness into the aching cluster of nerves in her groin.

She could feel her pussy pulsing like the drum beats of war. It was a powerful, insistent, natural impulse, like the powerful flow of the tides drug in and out by the moon's mighty call. It was begging to be released, opened up, and filled with the meaty cock of a beautiful man.

Releasing herself to the power of her pleasure, she pulled down her pants and underwear and threw them away across the room. They landed haphazardly on the hotel room's desk and knocked over the lamp.

She could feel Jean's breath, heavy, warm, and intense on her neck. He was lightly brushing his teeth over her skin, and she could feel they were pointed. His touches were becoming more aggressive and powerful, and less controlled. It thrilled her and she squealed with pleasure, as he viciously rubbed at her clitoris. His teeth grazing her neck were the perfect mix of gentle, tingling sensation and hinted danger.

His hand came off her breast, making her whimper and wish he hadn't stopped gripping her so tightly, but then he dove two thick fingers into her open, waiting vagina. His long fingers had no problem reaching and pumping her g-spot. She hopped up and down, the pleasure of his hands almost too great to sustain.

She had her eyes shut, but she felt the warm presence of Danver's body approach them. She opened her eyes to see him standing in front of them, staring down with a look of violent longing at her writhing body.

Then he sneered, as if something he saw filled him with rage.

But it was just the rage of passion and unfulfilled desire, because the next thing he did was tear Jean's hands out of Melanie's pussy, and to throw both of them backwards on the bed. Melanie's naked body lay prostrate on top of Jean's warm form. Danver dove on top of Melanie and inside her with a ferocious, leonine roar. Melanie screamed as he drove into her, ecstatic at the pleasure she was about to receive from his rough thrusting.

DANVER

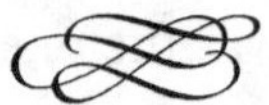

She was so tight that he worried for a second that he'd hurt her. But even the quickest of looks at her face told that she was screaming with pleasure. Her smile lit her up, changing every second like a gorgeous firework as her focus shifted between different sources of pleasure.

Jean purred as his hands fondled her breasts, squeezing tightly and toying with her nipples from his position underneath her. As Danver pumped forward, he moved both of them up and down, as if he was fucking them both.

Danver felt angry and jealous, watching Jean's hands on Melanie's plump, bouncing breasts. He growled and pulled off one of Jean's hands, gripping Melanie's breast possessively. Jean smiled at him knowingly, mocking his jealousy, and then he slid his hand down Melanie's body to her clitoris.

He rubbed her as best he could and as hard as he could manage. It was hard to keep a grip as Danver shoved his cock inside Melanie's beautiful, squirming body. She screamed so loud a small voice in the back of Danver's head wondered if someone was going to call a noise complaint.

But he wouldn't be able to stop, even if security stormed in ready for a fight. Nobody could tear him off Melanie now. Her pussy was so warm. Every inch of his massive cock felt squeezed so tightly, he felt like coming already. The thought of filling her warm vagina up with his burning semen made him howl.

He'd never felt like this before. Every glance at her body, so tan, smooth and strong underneath his relentless onslaught of thrusts, drove him wild all over again. And her beautiful face, with that ear-to-ear smile . . . Even though he was the one dominating her, the way she was grinning, you would think she was the predator who'd caught the perfect feast.

She screamed, "Yes, howl for me, fuck me into oblivion, fuck me until I split in half." He did as he was ordered. He was powerless not to.

There was no chance to control himself, when he felt her hard nipple responding to the rough caress of his calloused thumb. He couldn't breathe as he saw his throbbing, aching cock disappearing into the perfect curls of hair that surrounded her pussy. In the low light of the hotel room, her light brown hair looked like gold around her warm, pulsing vagina.

She screamed for him to fuck her harder, but he didn't have enough leverage like this. He was still sort of off the bed, and she was on top of Jean. Without exiting her, he picked her up so he was standing, with her wrapped around his waist. He gripped her hips viciously and pounded her into his hips as they thrust upward, doubling the force with which he was punching his massive cock inside her.

She screamed as if she was on a bumpy rollercoaster. Then she stopped screaming and her face froze into a delicious look of pleasure. It was as if she was frozen in time at the height of ecstasy.

She let loose a quiet, feminine whimper and clenched tightly around Danver. He kept pounding her as she came. Her orgasm rocked through her like lightning strikes, each pulse making her whole body spasm with a shriek as she called out for God.

When she stopped spasming and her shrieks turned to satisfied, pleasured moans, Danver slowed down. But she wasn't done with him yet.

Jean had taken off his jeans and underwear as he watched them fuck. He rubbed his cock the whole time. Danver followed Melanie's gaze to where Jean's massive hand rubbed up and down his member, squeezing tightly.

In a sultry, deep voice tinged with exhaustion, Melanie said "Jean, strip all the way down." He did as he was told. Melanie slid off Danver's cock with a final whimper and shiver through her body, as his cock rubbed her over-excited pussy on the way out.

She stood, naked and utterly gorgeous, and surveyed the two hard, naked werewolves before her.

"What should I do with you first?" she said, her voice dripping with erotic possibility.

Danver felt like a plaything. He couldn't look away from her. He knew if she ordered him to fight Jean to the death, he'd do it.

If she ordered him to get on his knees and suck Jean's cock, he'd do it. If it meant her beautiful face would light up with that gorgeous smile, he'd do anything. He felt more scared and utterly thrilled than he'd ever felt in his life.

She pointed at Jean and demanded, "Lay down on the bed with your cock up."

He tipped a deferential head. Clearly, he'd been taken in by the magic of her sexy allure as well. Once again, Danver wondered if he'd been bewitched, but he knew deep down, it was just her beauty and confidence that made him want to do anything she asked.

That and his pulsing cock, which wanted so badly to go back inside her pussy. He watched as she climbed on top of Jean, so her pussy was directly over his face.

With excitement, he began to lick her, and Danver felt the ache of jealous longing deep in his balls. He wanted to taste her so badly, but he wouldn't move until he was ordered to. As soon as Jean began licking her, Melanie smacked him viciously on the stomach. He let out a surprised gasp. She said, "Next time you do something without me telling you to, there will be claws."

"Yes. I'll be a good boy," he said with an excited purr.

She said, "Jean, I'm going to suck your cock." Danver's breathing deepened. He was looking at her ass, but she had her legs spread wide as if she was presenting herself. He could see her warm, wet pussy, open in front of him. She wriggled her ass, taunting him with her open holes.

She ordered, "Danver, fuck me hard from behind. While you fuck me, Jean will suck your balls. Don't go so fast Jean can't suck on you."

Danver didn't usually like doggy style. He worried the woman wouldn't enjoy it, or he might hurt her. But being ordered like this, he knew it was exactly what Melanie wanted, and that heightened his pleasure.

He climbed onto the bed with them and positioned himself over Jean's face. He slid inside Melanie again and abandoned himself to utter ecstasy.

He'd never had his balls licked before. It created a powerful jolt of pleasure that shot up his cock to the tip and even sent pleasure backwards, toward his asshole.

He felt as if Melanie was reading his mind, because in between her moans around a mouthful of Jean's massive cock, she commanded, "Jean, fuck Danver's ass with your finger."

His warm, thick fingers didn't explore Danver's ass gently. He shoved them inside, and fucked hard, as he was ordered. The pleasure of Melanie's vagina, and Jean's tongue on his balls and his fingers attacking his asshole, turned the whole bottom half of Danver's body into a thundercloud of pleasure. Melanie was screaming, her voice muffled by Jean's cock deep inside her throat. Even Jean was losing his customary composure, which thrilled Danver and made him feel more powerful. He put even more strength into his thrusts inside of Melanie, as Jean moaned and vibrated his balls.

He could feel they were glistening wet from the attentions of Jean's tongue. Melanie ordered, "Suck on him."

Jean wrapped one of Danver's balls inside his mouth and sucked. The combined thrill of all of his erogenous zones made Danver shout at the top of his lungs, until the wolf inside him took over, and he howled.

All three of them were shifting slightly. Just enough to add even more strength and raw animal power to their lovemaking. Danver couldn't call it anything else; not while he could feel his love for Melanie so strongly, and his love for Jean's love for Melanie, no matter how depraved their acts might have seemed on the surface.

Melanie came hard, writhing and ordering Jean to stop licking Danver and start licking her. Jean's face was battered by Melanie and Danver's thrusting hips, but he didn't stop adding pleasure to Melanie's throbbing clitoris.

She spasmed repeatedly with gorgeous screams, filled with intensity. Danver howled as her pussy squeezed his cock tighter than anything he'd ever felt before.

As she reached the end of her orgasm, she ordered, "Eiffel Tower me."

Danver didn't know what that meant. But he watched Jean smoothly rolled out from underneath the two of them, and took a position in front of her face. He shoved his cock into her mouth and began to fuck mercilessly.

She screamed and howled in equal measure. Danver followed suit, and the two men pounded both ends while she rubbed her clitoris with one hand. Her orgasming never stopped.

She took her mouth away from Jean only to say quickly, "Come in me. Fuck me until you both come deep inside me."

Danver would have been unsure. He would have been adamant about not doing that, at risk of impregnating a woman who already had a mate.

But he loved her deeply. He would do anything she ordered.

So he gripped his hands tightly on her hips, leaving bruises from how tightly he held her. He pounded her relentlessly, with no regard for how hard Jean was dominating her mouth and throat. Both men just did as they were ordered.

With massive, violent roars, and feeling the screams and quivering of a still-orgasming Melanie, both men spurted hot werewolf come into her. Danver felt as if his whole self was spilling out into her, until she contained everything he ever wanted and ever could be.

Shaking, and soaked with sweat on a creaking bed that had been damaged by their powerful rutting, the three stood for a moment without moving. Melanie breathed heavily and raggedly around Jean's cock as the blood left it.

Then both men exited her, and she collapsed to the bed. Danver looked at her spent, exhausted form, and found the curve of her spine and the lines of her legs to be works of art. She curled up like a happy puppy after too much play and smiled like a saint in heaven.

Danver's come leaked out from her vagina and pooled on her legs and the bed. She wriggled her hips, enjoying its wet warmth. Jean's come glistened on her lips in the few places it had escaped during his vigorous mouth-fucking. After swallowing the come and licking her lips, Melanie said with a contented sigh, "I have never felt more beautiful than I do right now."

Then her gorgeous eyes fluttered closed, and she laid her head back and laughed weakly and joyfully.

Danver said softly, "You're the most beautiful thing I've ever seen in my life."

Jean was staring at the ceiling in a daze. His mustache glistened with ball sweat and saliva. Finally, he said, "Well, that was fun. Though I'm not sure I could survive more. But hell, you only live once, who's ready for round two?"

Melanie laughed and said, "I can't move. You've paralyzed me. I am nothing but one fluttery good vibe. I don't even have the energy for multiple vibes. Just the one good one."

Danver looked at them both and shook his head. He felt like crying. His soul had left his body and gone into Melanie's keeping, forever.

It was what he always dreamed finding his true mate would feel like.

"Was this a game for you two?" he asked.

Melanie's eyes popped open. She didn't move, but she threw a glance at Danver. She frowned.

"Of course not," she said, "It was wonderful. Spiritual."

Her voice was soft, and the aching feelings there almost brought

Danver to tears. But Jean interjected, "If it was a game, there would be winners and losers. I'd say we all won, wouldn't you?"

The smug look on his face made Danver want to tear it off with one swipe of his claws. But instead of doing that, he took one last look at Melanie's heavenly form, headed for the window, and jumped out.

He was a wolf before he hit the ground. He didn't need any of the items they left behind. They were all just stuff.

He was leaving his heart behind, anyway. Nothing else mattered now.

MELANIE

*J*ean swooped into the seat across from her as Melanie tried her best to be soothed by familiar sights and sounds. After all, before her current pack, she'd lived in and around Seattle for a long time. But the smell of coffee failed to soothe, and the hipster folk music the coffee shop was pumping too loudly agitated her.

"It is time for me to try some of Seattle's famous coffee," Jean said with playful solemnity.

He took a deep sniff and, then, as if he was tasting wine, he sipped and bit and swished it in his mouth. Unlike proper wine tasting, he swallowed.

Melanie wished she had the emotional energy to be amused. "What's the verdict?" she asked.

He nodded thoughtfully. "It is exactly like all other coffee I have ever had."

Melanie didn't laugh. She couldn't. Her mind was in two very sad places.

In one place, she was waiting for a phone call from a powerful vampire, who had her mate and who threatened her son's freedom.

There was nothing worse she could imagine than her son becoming a vampire's thrall. She'd kill him before she let him submit to that.

That thought burned so brightly in her head, that she wouldn't let the vampire take her son alive, that she shuddered and had to clamp her eyes shut to breathe. It was so hard to retain control and not shift when she was this anxious. She wished they were in a less-crowded place, or even better, out in the woods where she could run off some steam. But she needed her phone on her when the vampire called. She kept it on the table, hoping they weren't smart or paranoid enough to track which cell tower it connected with when she answered. If they did, they would know she was in Seattle, tracking them. Prey knowing you were after it was only good if they scared easy. It worked well on rabbits, and made them make bad decisions. It wouldn't work well on a vampire.

The other place her mind kept going zo, was wherever Danver was. He'd made love to her (and Jean) and then abandoned her. She knew it was more complicated than that, but her feelings couldn't help but be sore.

Jean watched her carefully and asked, "Which of your many woes and worries is concerning you at present?"

She tried to smile, but it came out more of a sneering smirk. She said, "All of them. But I'm upset we're down a soldier right before the siege."

Jean shrugged. His casual responses were starting to grate on Melanie, but she couldn't risk him running off, too. She needed at least one other werewolf to watch her back.

"I am sure if you asked nicely, he would come back." he said.

Melanie tilted her head and looked at him with confusion. "What do you mean, asked nicely? He left his phone in the room. I can't call him. He's in wolf form, and probably a hundred miles away by now."

Jean threw his hands up into the air. "I must be being silly, then. But it seemed as if, last night at least, you didn't even have to ask nicely, and he did things he would otherwise never do. Only because you asked him and because it would make you happy."

Melanie thought this over for a long time. Then, she said slowly and quietly, "Do you think he's in love with me?"

Jean shook his head. "It is more. Love explains some of it. Not all."

Melanie said, "It can't be a werewolf bond. We're a pack, but just being pack wouldn't mean he was beholden to follow my orders. I can still feel my mate bond with Carl. As angry as I am with him, he's still alive, and we haven't broken the bond."

Jean pretended to muse by putting his chin in his hand. "Hmm, what could there possibly be in werewolf culture where one werewolf must listen to the other? I simply can't think of anything at all."

Melanie glared at him. "Women can't be alphas. It doesn't happen."

Jean smirked and said very quietly, so the humans couldn't hear it over the music, "Last night I sucked a man's balls for your pleasure. And it felt so, so right. Either you're an alpha, or I've discovered a new side of myself that loves being the submissive one." He cocked his head to the side thoughtfully. "Maybe that's it. It *was* rather fun."

Melanie said, "An alpha can't force someone to do what they want. The pack just agrees to follow their leadership."

Jean rolled his eyes. "I'm not saying you forced us or brainwashed us. I'm saying we did what you said because we wanted to; because it felt good. And because you seemed more powerful than us. What does that sound like?"

Melanie shook her head. "That's too much to think about right now. I've never heard of a female alpha. It didn't keep Danver from running away."

Jean pointed out, "Because you didn't ask him to stay. If you called him, now, he'd come back to you."

Melanie considered the power of that. She frowned. "No. If he wants to abandon me, so be it. He made his choice. Now, I've got hard ones of my own to make."

Almost on cue, her phone rang. Her heart stuttered and skipped, and then sped up immensely. Werewolf heartbeats were already incredibly fast, and her chest hurt from the powerful anxiety that filled her. She clicked on answer.

The voice on the other end was filled with power, though it was raspy like parchment rubbed together.

"Did you collect what you owe?"

Melanie took a deep breath and, according to the plan she had worked out with Jean and Danver before he took off, said firmly, "Yes. It was a fucking challenge, but we did it. Where do I meet you?"

The voice on the line only laughed and said, "We will be in touch." Then the line went dead.

* * *

ON THE APPROACH to the vampire hangout, Jean had tried to assure Melanie that all was well. At least, as well as possible, considering the circumstances.

He said, "They're trying to scare you. Vampires like this love fear. Not all vampires, mind you. Most just want to be left alone to live their lives, uh, live their deaths, I suppose, in peace. But this guy is clearly trying to increase your anxiety and fear before taking the money. He wants you scared. That's why the wait."

Melanie snarled, "Or it's because they're going to my house right now to attack my family."

Jean said, "It is unlikely. You say you have the money. He probably thinks you do not have the money. What he really wants is Michael as a thrall. But he must play with you, until you admit you do not have the money. That is what he wants. For you to be so scared, then you come clean and give him Michael."

Melanie said, "Well he's going to be waiting a damned long time."

They were standing outside the hideout. It was like any other suburban house in this pleasing Washington neighborhood, except all of the lights were off. Melanie could see shapes moving around inside. There were beings in there, alright. Just beings who liked to keep the lights off.

Jean had explained a few things about the vampires he'd come across before. They were interested in staying out of sight, and out of mind. If they were unaware that someone knew their secret, they wouldn't consider them a threat.

The plan was for Jean to go right up to the front door and pretend to be a neighbor. Someone in the neighborhood who'd lost a cat. Meanwhile, Melanie would stalk around outside, trying to get a sense for how many people were inside. She'd also try to use her mate bond to detect Carl.

If they could get Carl back, the vampires would have less leverage. The family would still owe them, and would have to go into hiding – unless Carl relinquished his claim on Michael. That would mean he'd have to sever ties with the family.

Melanie tried not to think about that. They'd been together for so long. They'd managed a miracle and bred a beautiful child together. She didn't know if she could just let Carl disappear from her life forever. From Michael's life. If Carl relinquished his claim, as Michael's father, then by werewolf law he was never permitted to speak to him again.

It was a shameful state for a werewolf male. He would be known as an abandoner, which was a huge werewolf sin. You didn't leave your mate and child without your protection.

Jean put on his best friendly American male face and voice, which was considerably different from his usual attitude. It was a goofier, brighter sort of guy. Melanie kind of liked it. She realized that he was acting how Danver acted like when he was in a good, friendly mood. Which was rare these days.

She ignored that thought, too. She cleared her mind, feeling for the ever-present mate bond that would let her sense if Carl were near. She was wearing jogging clothes and she stretched in a position by the vampire's fence, partially hidden by the neighbor's shrubs.

The hope was that if anybody saw her lurking on the road, she would look like a jogger taking a stretch break and not a stalker. Of course, if the vampires knew what she looked like, then her leggings and step-counting wristband wouldn't be enough of a disguise, but hopefully humans would leave her alone. If anybody looked as if they were staring at her, she'd just take a jog around the block, but stay near enough the house that if things went really south, and Jean howled, she could help. But he seemed to think he wouldn't need any help, even if things went badly.

Melanie was beginning to realize that Jean was a little scarier than he seemed when you were talking with him. If he was so sure of himself around these vampires, he must be very powerful and talented.

She scolded herself for letting her mind wander so much. Jean was already inside, putting his life at risk. The least she could do was figure whether if Carl was there. She shut her eyes and stretched, touching her toes and reaching up high as is she was cooling down after a section of her run. She reached out her awareness and tugged on the mate bond, calling Carl to her. If he was trapped, but nearby, she would be able to tell by the response of his energy on the bond.

Her tug tightened the bond, and she felt Carl move closer to her. The fact that she could even tell, showed he was nearby. So he was in the house.

But then the bond slackened. It hit her with a jolt of pain and she opened her eyes.

He couldn't come to her. She couldn't tell if he was choosing to ignore her or if he'd tried to answer but had been restrained.

When she opened her eyes, a woman was standing before her. She was sleek and tall, with impossibly long black hair and dead eyes.

"Looking for something? Or should I say, someone?" the woman asked in a deep voice that was full vowels that sounded like a slight accent.

Melanie yawned and said, "Just looking for a runner's high."

The vampire woman did not believe her. "Clearly," she said sarcastically. Before Melanie could get into a battle stance, the woman reached out.

Melanie didn't know if it was magic or a physical hit that brought her down. She wasn't awake long enough to figure it out. She only had enough time, before she lost consciousness from the pain, to hope that Jean had gotten out.

And then, feeling like a fool, she whispered for Danver to come to her.

DANVER

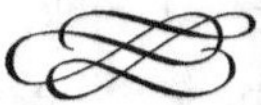

*D*anver was trying to shake off the terrible shock he'd gotten earlier. He'd heard Melanie's voice in his ear, whispering for him. He was convinced he was hearing things, going crazy.

He needed some time to clear his mind and think. That was easier in wolf form.

There was something very simple and soothing about the hunt. Danver didn't like hunting traditional prey. Anyone could kill a deer, if you caught up with it. It was harder to kill other predators. It required more focus. More violence, yes, but at least it was the violence of an equal lashing back out at you.

Wes thought he was crazy for going after poisonous snakes and climbing trees to stalk owls. He wondered if the extra effort was worth it. Danver felt that the easy kill wasn't worth it. He'd tried to explain that to Wes, but he'd never understood not taking the path of least resistance. Melanie had understood, and nodded approvingly whenever Danver expressed the sentiment.

Danver narrowed his focus on the large animal in front of him. It was about a hundred feet directly ahead. He made sure he was standing where the wind wouldn't carry his scent easily.

He stepped forward slowly, testing the awareness of his quarry. He couldn't tell exactly what it was. It was big like a bear, but shaped like a . . . wolf. Was it another werewolf? Wolves could get that big up north. He tried to smell the creature, but it was too far away.

He cursed his human brain for interfering with the sacred cleansing that was the hunt. When his wolf brain took over, he felt at peace. Whole.

He couldn't jump out on and fight another werewolf. That was murder, and the werewolf's pack would be after him forever in a blood feud. He howled. If it was a werewolf, it would alert him to his presence. If it was a bear, it probably wouldn't care; not realizing it was being hunted.

It turned around and looked straight at Danver. Definitely another werewolf. He could tell from the burning eyes. It was pitch black, except for white paws, like a tuxedo cat. A strange print for a wolf.

Danver walked forward baring his teeth, but not growling. He ducked his head in a gesture of non-violence. He wasn't looking to fight another werewolf.

His own light-blond hair was better suited for sand or snow than for this forest, so he knew the other werewolf must see him. How strange to come across a fellow shifter so deep in the woods.

The other werewolf howled back and in a surprising gesture of trust and goodwill, started to shift back to human. In only a moment, it became clear to Danver why the wolf had trusted him. Danver bared his teeth and growled viciously.

"I come bearing a message from your Alpha," Jean yelled, cupping his hands around his mouth to shout. "Do you reject it? Or do you want to kill the messenger?"

That was nothing like anything Danver had expected him to say. He snarled, mostly reflexively, because he hated Jean so much. He walked forward, not willing to come out of wolf form, yet. He waited for Jean to explain what the hell he meant.

Jean moved toward him, strolling with a casual stride, but heading straight for Danver. He looked like he had a big joke to share. He was stifling a smile.

When they were only ten feet from each other, Danver looked

straight into Jean's face and growled. He wanted Jean to hurry up and explain why he was here.

Jean got the message. With a little mock bow, he said, "As I said, I'm only the messenger. I suppose it's not a direct message. I can only assume your alpha has sent for you by now, given the current predicament."

Danver's head tilted, one ear up. He waited for Jean to stop fooling around and actually tell him something.

Jean said, "Have you not heard a message?"

Danver's lips quivered off his teeth, but then he stopped his snarling, threatening expression. Because he had heard something; he had heard Melanie calling for him. He shifted as quickly as he could, without risking damaging his body. As soon as his vocal cords were arranged for him to speak, he said to Jean, "What's happened to Melanie?"

Jean shook his head. "What do you think happened, you dummy? We went to the vampires. She got captured. Plain and simple."

Before Jean could say anything else, Danver was right next to him. Danver gripped his throat and lifted him off the ground. He was gratified to see Jean finally looked a little uncomfortable, although he was still smiling, damn him.

Danver growled, "What the hell happened? Why didn't you protect her?"

Jean choked out, "You know what the plan was. We didn't want the vampires to know I was there with Melanie. They took her without me knowing. When I came out, she was gone. They must have her. But I know where they're keeping her."

Danver dropped Jean, who landed gracefully with a small cough. "You are lucky I am not a proud man. Or I would tear out your belly for this insult," he said with a half-sneer, half-smile.

Danver retorted, "A proud man would not have left a woman in the hands of vampires."

"And what did you do, exactly?" Jean retorted. "Other than run away when she needed you most?"

Danver roared and plunged his fist into a tree. It splintered.

Jean rolled his eyes. "Please, do stop being so dramatic. I came here, so you could help me recover Melanie. And maybe that Carl of hers, although I am more inclined to leave him behind at this point. He seems like, how they say, quite a piece of work."

Danver felt too many emotions fighting for dominance. Embarrassment, pride, confusion, rage, and jealousy; all bubbling and warring inside of him. He wanted to fall to his knees. But his instincts were still up about Jean. He didn't want to show too much weakness.

Jean had already figured out his primary weak spot was Melanie. He didn't want to put himself into a more vulnerable position.

Danver growled, "Why are you helping us? Why come all the way out here and put yourself into harm's way? Is it just to sleep with Melanie? Because you did that, so you can fuck off now."

Jean looked at Danver with some surprise. Danver didn't usually curse, and losing his temper wasn't his style.

Danver felt that many things had changed completely, since he'd been inside Melanie. His life was forever muddled up, and he just wanted some time to figure it out. But it had been selfish of him to take that time now, he realized that.

He needed the answer to his question. He clarified more calmly, "Before I run back into battle with you, and with Melanie's life at risk, I have to know why I should trust you."

Jean shrugged. Danver wanted to rip his arms off. Jean said with exasperation, "I told you. I'm a vampire hunter. There's a bounty for vampires who engage in illegal activity or violent acts against werewolves. This is what I do for a living."

Danver stepped toward him with a violent heart. "Then why did you leave Melanie instead of killing the vampires?"

Jean held his ground. "Because I'm good at my job. I know when I'll win. I wouldn't win going up against fifteen vampires alone, and there are no fewer than fifteen vampires in that house. Give or take a few thralls; I might be off on my count, because the thralls dress and start to look as dead as their hosts. But even humans can carry weapons, and if they're guarding werewolves, they might have silver bullets."

Danver said, "How did you find Melanie? How did you get sent here by the agency?"

Jean looked annoyed by Danver's suspicions, finally showing a crack in his nonchalance. He said, "The same reason you used the agency. I am a lonely man. I have no pack and no family; no mate. I was looking for a powerful mate, who would be my partner in the hunt for bad vampires. That is why I matched with Melanie, I am sure. She is very powerful, as you have seen."

"You're telling me you signed up for the service for normal reasons, but coincidentally, you matched with someone who needed help with a vampire?" Danver said with as much threat dripping from his voice as he could manage.

Jean threw his hands up to the air, utterly exasperated by Danver. "I cannot explain the strange turnings of fate! All I can tell you is that vampires hate werewolves. They love turning us into their lifelong servants and abusing us. It's probably because our ancestors hunted them down and slaughtered them by the hundreds, but I would not want to conjecture."

Danver looked into Jean's eyes, trying to detect how much truth was in his phrases. It was possible he had been in league with the vampires the entire time.

Jean held Danver's gaze and said, "The vampires are becoming bolder. They love preying on smaller packs. You and your family would not have remained unmolested for long."

Danver sneered, "They're not my family. I'm an interloper."

Jean said gently, "It is often that family is found, rather than given. From what I have seen, they are your family."

Danver couldn't find any lies in the eyes of his rival. He wanted to, he realized. Deep down, he hoped there was a reason this man wasn't fit to be around Melanie.

Jean said, "I know you need to gain confidence in me, but I am afraid every second we stand here staring into each other's eyes, is another second they could be hurting Melanie."

Danver frowned, but he nodded. Jean was right. They needed to get going.

"Are you and I partners in this thing, here?" Jean asked.

Danver couldn't let one thing go. Before they returned, he had to settle this last problem.

He said, "I'll trust you as my partner in rescuing Melanie, if you answer two questions for me honestly."

Jean groaned, and quipped, "I have nearly reached my honesty limit for the day, thank you very much. But please, ask away. You're worse than the American census takers when they knock on your door. So nosy."

Danver demanded, "If we rescue Melanie and return her and Carl to safety in our pack, will you cease pursuing her?"

Jean said without hesitation, "Oh, my friend, I ceased my pursuit of her when I saw the two of you together. I care not for Carl and his desires, however much you cloak your own in concerns for the holy state of matehood. But in essence, yes, I promise to stop pursuing Melanie as my mate. Or rather, not to restart my attempts. Unless you are asking me to specifically stop screwing her?"

Danver snarled. Jean quickly said, "Ah, yes, well, I will cease that activity as well. You're welcome. What is the second question?"

Danver asked, "Are you trying to join our pack?"

Jean thought for a moment. He said, "Honestly, I had been considering the task at hand in a very focused manner. I had not thought of joining your ragtag band. It is not a large pack, though it does have a bit of land. New Mexico is rather warm for me. No, I do not think I will join. Unless you move somewhere much more pleasant in the summer." He smiled brightly. "There. Are you as satisfied as I can make you without licking your balls?"

Danver swiped at Jean with a roar. Jean deftly sidestepped it and said, "But a joke! So touchy. Shall we go?"

Without waiting for an answer, Jean shifted and took off running. Danver followed suit, having to push himself to keep up. Jean was an impressive wolf in many ways.

He was powerful, and Danver trusted his answers had been truthful. That didn't mean he had to like the guy.

MELANIE

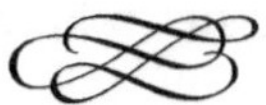

Melanie woke up in chains, strapped to a wall with her legs splayed. They had her standing up in an uncomfortable position. For a human, it would have been unbearable, because all of the pressure was either on the core, to stand flush with the wall, or on the joints if you let the chains hold you up.

Thanks to her werewolf-strength muscles, Melanie was fine as far as that went. The only uncomfortable thing was how the manacles bit into her arms. They felt horrible against her flesh.

She twisted her neck to look at them, and gasped at what she saw. They were silver handcuffs and chains. No wonder they hurt like hell. She wouldn't be able to break out of them, and she wouldn't be able to shift while she was in them. Silver totally negated her powers and much of her strength. Plus it stung like a bitch.

She looked down to see if her ankles were clasped with the same material. They were, but they weren't touching her bare skin, so didn't hurt as badly. The vampires had left her jogging attire on, which Melanie was surprised to see. They probably hadn't wanted to risk her waking up by undressing her. They had likely had to hurry to get her into the silver chains in what she could only assume was the basement, judging by the total lack of light. Her eyes had no problem in the pitch darkness, though.

Leaving her clothes on gave added a tiny obstacle to shifting. It was more uncomfortable to do clothed, because the shift was already an uncomfortable process. Having to burst through clothes was another hindrance. If it wasn't for the silver manacles, though, that wouldn't have slowed Melanie down much at all. But, she couldn't shift as long as she was held by the silver. Maybe she could shift her face and bite somebody, but as satisfying as that was, it wouldn't help her much.

Two vamps entered. A man and a woman, neither of whom looked very old. They both looked pale and haggard, like models from the 90s, when everyone was into that heroin chic look. They had stringy, lank hair and protruding cheekbones. They might have been beautiful in life, but in death, they looked like . . . well . . . death. They looked as if a hard kick to the sternum would make them evaporate into ash.

Melanie itched for a chance to try her theory. Life on the ranch and in her old pack had been pretty peaceful. No pack wars to fight or blood feuds to avenge. She loved to hunt, and she'd forgotten how much she loved battle. Maybe she could goad these two string beans into fighting her.

Melanie snarled, "I thought vampires were supposed to be hot. You two look like Halloween decorations."

The vampires laughed – a breathy strained affair that was difficult to listen to. It sounded as if expelling air through their throats hurt them.

The male vamp said with a leering sneer, "We're young. Give us time to feed and plump up. You look plump enough to eat already, doggie."

The female vamp laughed and echoed, "Doggie, doggie, wag your tail," in a taunting, singsong voice. Melanie growled.

The vamps stepped closer. The guy said, "Ooh, so scary, doggie. But we know you can't do shit."

The female vamp echoed him again, with a horrible sneer, "You can't do shit, you stupid animal."

The guy continued, "Because I don't know if you noticed yet, but you're bound in silver. That means you can't shift. You can't break free. You're at our mercy."

The female giggled childishly, which felt freaky coming from what looked like a dead forty-year-old model. "We don't have a whole lot of mercy. For anybody. Especially a monster like you."

Melanie sneered, "At least I'm alive. You're an aberration. A demon, except not as cool. Demons are tougher. Vamps just need one tap in the chest. From wood. Not even anything that's hard to find. A simple stick of wood. I could take a kitchen chair and kill you."

The man swiped a quick smack across Melanie's face. She didn't see it coming, but it stung like hell.

Good, she was pissing them off. The girl looked livid. They wanted her scared and she wasn't about to give them the satisfaction, even if she was freaking out on the inside.

She was glad werewolf hearts were fast normally. They would be able to hear her quick heartbeat, but they wouldn't be able to tell it was faster than usual because of her fear.

Stepping closer to Melanie, the girl hissed, "You're the aberration. Half dog, half person."

The man smirked, flexing the hand that had whipped across Melanie's face with such force. "I wonder how that happened. Wonder which one of your ancestors fucked a dog."

Melanie squinted at the man. "Which one of your ancestors fucked a komodo dragon? Because you've got that skin texture and tone. Big family resemblance."

The vamp lunged forward and bared his teeth. The blackness of his open mouth was like an abyss of hell, gaping open toward her with pointed, snake-like teeth.

He hissed, "Enough bantering, you silly plaything. We're here to feed on you. To grow strong on werewolf blood."

Melanie lunged back at him, snapping her own teeth, which had grown longer and sharper. He stepped back.

Melanie growled, "You think I'm the mongrel offspring of ancient bestiality, and yet you're still going to drink me? What does that make you? A fucking leech."

The vampire growled and lunged forward to feed, but in his rage he didn't pay great attention to his approach. He was young, and not as educated as the other, Melanie guessed. Because an older vampire would know that the first thing to shift, and the fastest, was a were-wolf's mouth.

In the split-second it took him to lunge, Melanie's snout and slathering maw grew out of her face. She chomped around the vampire's neck before he could get to hers. As he screamed and hissed in panic, she shook her head, as she did when a rabbit or possum was still fighting in its death throes.

You can't kill a vampire by breaking their neck. But you can disconnect their nerve endings so they're paralyzed until one of their magic-inclined brethren witchcraft them back together.

Melanie clenched and shook, ignoring the slashes and beatings to her torso and head from the female vamp. She shook until she heard the sickening snap that she was waiting for. She opened her mouth which was covered in the stale, coagulated blood of the vamp, and he slumped to the floor.

The girl vamp hissed at her and screamed, "Stupid bitch!"

Melanie's face was fully-shifted. She roared and lunged forward. The girl vamp had backed up too much for Melanie to reach her, but she noticed with satisfaction that the vamp jumped back another few feet, to be sure. She grabbed her fallen compatriot by the feet and pulled him to the other side of the room. He screamed at her, "Go get Marwenn!" He screamed it over and over.

Marwenn must be the magic vamp that had captured Melanie in the first place, she reasoned. She opened her mouth, trying to drool out the horrible taste of the vampire's dead blood. Vampire was abso-lutely the worst taste ever, every werewolf knew that.

The female vamp ran upstairs, leaving her screaming and whim-pering compatriot behind. He cursed and swore at Melanie, who was glad he didn't have any magic. If he did, she'd be in a hell of a lot more trouble than she already was, and his broken neck wouldn't matter.

Melanie knew she had a chance to escape in the two to three minutes it would take for the magical vampire to get down here. Once that happened, Melanie was screwed.

The silver burned like hell and kept her from doing her shift. It sapped much of her strength, as well. She felt fatigued from breaking the vamp's neck and performing even just the shift of her face.

So her arms didn't have any of her usual strength. But they were their usual size for her human shape, which meant they were small.

That meant she was going to have to do something that would hurt like hell. But if she didn't, and that magic vampire came down here, she'd probably put her through something worse than hell.

Melanie began twisting her hand to pull it out of the manacle. The silver rubbed her skin raw and burnt it, causing it to both bleed and sear. The smell of her own sizzling flesh was repulsive.

She twisted and pulled at her wrist until finally, blessedly, it popped through. Slowly, she felt her usual healing powers start to activate. Couldn't happen fast enough, the silver burns hurt like hell.

She did the same with the other manacle, stifling the urge to howl at the pain. She looked down at her feet. These would be harder.

But the top of her could shift. She effected the change as quickly as she could, and her legs stayed stuck in a weird half-place between woman and wolf, and still restrained by the silver in the manacles that clasped her ankles.

In this strange, uncomfortable form, and with the paralyzed vampire screaming at her from the ground and yelling for Marwenn to stop her, Melanie reached up as high as she could and gripped an exposed ceiling beam. She hoped it could support her weight.

She held it and, with every bit of strength she could muster, she pulled up with her massive werewolf biceps, fighting the restraints' hold on her feet. Finally, in the same way she'd slipped out of her wrist manacles, she slipped away from the feet cuffs.

Utterly free, but with her wrists and ankles horribly scarred, she noticed the healing was going slowly, and even stopping. She wondered if she'd ever be free of the scarred reminder of the vampire's silver. Not daring to stop to ask that question, she pulled herself up toward the ceiling. The floor was made of wood. Her wolf grinned in a horrible leer.

"I hear someone's been a big, bad wolf." She heard from the basement steps. It was Marwenn the magic user.

Melanie wasn't going to wait around to see what she had in store for her. With a powerful roar, Melanie punched her way through the wooden ceiling.

She could see light from the first floor and she heard the confused shouts of the vampires in whatever room she was entering. She might be going out of the frying pan into the fire, but she sure as hell didn't want to deal with whatever Marwenn could cook up.

She pulled herself through and leaped up into the center of the vampire's living room. She was surrounded by six vamps. From their positions and expressions, they'd been having afternoon tea.

Melanie howled, and, in her bipedal werewolf form, showed them all what she had in her hand. A chunk of the wooden floor she'd just burst through. It was perfectly shaped to stake someone through the heart. She made her intentions clear by pointing at every vampire's chest in turn. She heard Marwenn's voice screaming for them to stop her, as the vampire made her way back upstairs.

Melanie was just going to get the hell out of there. She could see the front window, and knew she could dive through and run through the neighborhood in full wolf form. They wouldn't be able to catch her outside, in full view of the neighbors. But she felt that frantic tugging from the next room. Her mate bond screamed out to her.

She pulled on it, answering it as wolf, and hoping her mate would shift as well, so they could escape together. Then, she noticed the vampires were forming a circle around her. They planned on trapping her until Marwenn could deal with her.

Melanie picked the one who looked weakest. She knew the rules of the hunt. The skinniest, sickliest prey is the one who gets picked off.

She charged him and slammed the stake into his chest. He fell to the ground in a puff of dust. The keening wail of the other vampires seeing him collapse and disintegrate was horrific to hear with Melanie's improved werewolf senses. She made it into the next room, as the vampires reeled from her assault on their own. She finally found Carl.

He wasn't tied up. He wasn't even guarded by anything she could see. But he had shifted, and he looked ready to run away with her. He whimpered in his full wolf form and held his head down in a gesture of submissive apology. Melanie growled and completed her shift to full wolf.

Marwenn strolled into the room and placed herself between them and the window, through which Melanie had hoped to escape. Two other vampires followed her, large men with stern, deadly faces.

Marwenn began to work magic with a fluid gesture of movements. Melanie did not know the spell, or any spell, but she felt this must be the end for her. There was death in every movement, every curve, and every displacement of air Marwenn left.

A form from the front yard hurtled into the room through the window. Then another form, only a second behind it. They landed on top of the three vampires, who screamed and writhed in shock and pain.

It was blond wolf and a black one with white feet. Melanie recognized Danver's wolf, and figured the other was Jean. They mutilated the vampires, but all the werewolves knew this was only a brief distraction. Melanie and Carl made their way out of the now broken front window and burst into a supernaturally fast sprint through the suburbs.

Melanie could feel Danver following through the pack bonds. She knew that meant Jean got out as well. Danver was too good a person to leave anyone behind.

Together, the four wolves made their way toward the forest, where they could disappear and regroup deep in the mountains. Vampires weren't skilled trackers like werewolves were. If they got far enough, they'd hopefully be out of their reach.

Unless Marwenn was a seer as well as a skilled magician. Then they were fucked.

Melanie tried to subdue her anxious thoughts in the exhilaration of running in her wolf form. She tried to enjoy the adrenaline that came after a battle fought and won. But she knew there would be consequences. She had damaged the hive and killed one of their own. They weren't likely to give up on killing or capturing her family now.

Plus, now that Carl was back, what could she tell him to explain Jean's presence? And would she tell him about Danver?

It was strange that through it all, she felt a keen, brilliant joy whenever she caught sight of Danver's blond fur running in a beautiful streak beside her. Though the fear fought for control of her brain, knowing that he came back to save her gave her immense pleasure, and even joy, in this horrible crisis.

She knew that whatever happened next, she'd do whatever she needed to do to keep Michael safe, and to keep Danver by her side.

MELANIE

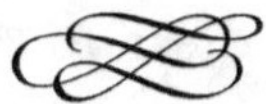

Danver and Jean went off into the woods to hunt for breakfast. At least, that's what they said they were doing. Melanie knew they were giving her and Carl time to talk.

They'd stayed in wolf form for the rest of the day and night, running into the mountains until dawn. By this point, they'd probably made their way out of Washington and into Oregon, possibly into Northern California. They'd stayed far away from roads and kept to the mountains and reservations, where a big wolf wouldn't cause alarm.

Their sense of geography was good, but not as good as a GPS. They'd need to shift back into human form soon and find some clothes, so they could go ask a human where the hell they were, and how far it was to New Mexico.

Melanie missed Wes. He knew how to hotwire a car, at least. She didn't know if any of the wolves she was with knew how, although maybe Jean did.

Melanie shifted, anger and nervousness taking an equal part. The shift was difficult. In tense situations, the werewolf body tended to want to stay in the more powerful, scarier, toothier form.

Carl didn't shift. He stared sullenly at the fire. She looked him over, inspecting his speckled brown fur for any signs of damage. She looked at her own wrists and ankles and found she was still scarred. She hated to look at it. She figured that if the vampires had done anything to Carl, they'd have used silver, and she'd be able to see if the wounds were still there, but he had no marks. No scars, not even a shaved spot where they possibly tortured him.

With a steel edge to her voice, she said, "Carl. Shift so you can talk to me."

He obeyed. Even in human form, he kept his downcast eyes aimed at the patch of dirt he'd been staring at.

Her voice quavering slightly, Melanie said, "Now you've got to do the talking part."

He said, "You think you know everything, I'm sure."

"Everything about what?" she said quietly.

"Everything about me," Carl shouted, suddenly bursting forth in uncharacteristic rage. "About what a fuck-up I am. I'm the male, God damn it, I should be protecting the family, right? Our family. What a joke. We're nothing but tagalongs for Cassidy and Wes's cozy little set-up. They get the master bedroom and we get a converted den."

"That's what you want to talk about?" Melanie said incredulously. "Rooms at the ranch? Because we talked about this, all of us, already. You and I get two rooms, one for your video games and computers and shit, the other for our bedroom, but Cassidy and Wes get the bigger room. That was the trade."

He kept going as if he couldn't hear her. "At least in Seattle, I was one of equals. I wasn't some unwanted relation. People respected me. I had friends. But I gave it all up and followed you."

Melanie said, "You didn't give up anything, Carl. It looks as if you've been living life exactly the way you wanted for a very long time."

Carl kept yelling. Melanie wished he would quiet down, or a hiker or something might notice two naked people yelling at each other in the forest. Or Danver would come back and beat his ass for yelling at her. That didn't sound so awful, at this point.

Carl shouted, "You don't get it. Nobody loves me there. Nobody cares about me. You're ashamed of me. But when I met Lara, she thought I was interesting. She laughed at me. No, she laughed with me, when I wanted her to. She laughed at my jokes. She didn't think I was the joke, like you and Wes do."

Melanie said softly, "I've never laughed at you, Carl. And I always told Wes to hold his tongue."

Carl nodded sarcastically. "That's what a man needs. His mate fighting his battles for him."

Melanie couldn't take that. "Oh, sorry, let me go put you back with the fucking vampires, then. You can fight your own way out."

Carl said, "I'm not talking about that! I was never going to be the alpha. Of any pack. But at home, in Seattle, at least people don't treat me like an unwanted pest. You all think I'm lazy, that I don't do my share on the ranch . . ."

Melanie snarled. "That's because you don't. That's because you sit on your ass."

Carl screeched, "So what? So I'd rather hang out than do stupid, unnecessary shit with horses. We're werewolves. We don't need to work. That's the whole freaking point of being a magical monster creature, right? We can just do whatever we want!"

"Like selling our son in exchange for gambling money?" Melanie said, tears choking her voice. "Is that what you wanted to do? What you think you had the right to do?"

Carl stopped dead. "I knew you were going to throw that right in my face." he said waveringly.

Melanie groaned. "Yes, Carl! I'm going to bring that up. Because I can't think of a single worse thing anyone has ever done in my entire life!"

Carl shouted, "How about you flirting with that Danver guy? Every day I had to watch him making eyes at you. The chemistry, as if he was going to mount you right in front of me. I had nightmares about it."

Melanie said with some awkwardness, "We're not talking about that right now. We're talking about the fact that a hive of vampires, including an Ancient One, currently think they own our pup."

Carl looked at her and said, "While I was gone, did you fuck him?"

Melanie screamed and took a violent step toward Carl. "For God's sake Carl, take responsibility for yourself, for once in your life!"

He looked at her tensely. He struggled with his words, trying to restrain his own mouth. Finally he said, "You're right. This is my fault. I was irresponsible, and it put our child in danger." He seemed surprised with himself for saying it aloud. He added, "This is all my fault. There's no excuse. I'm sorry."

His eyes were wide with shock. He stared at her, trembling at his words. Melanie closed the distance between him and cried into his chest.

She said, "He loves you so much. He loves you more than he loves me. My pup loves you more than he loves me, and you betrayed him. He'd do anything for you."

Carl held her tightly and stroked her hair as she cried. He apologized over and over, as if the words were being pulled out of him by a force outside his control. Melanie hugged him tight and cried.

It felt so good to be with her mate. Yet, when she reached for the bond, to feel that magical sense of comfort, it didn't respond joyously. It felt tight, strained. It was easy to break, because it was so weak. She left it alone and stepped back from Carl's embrace.

"Now that we've established this is your fault, what the hell are we going to do about it?" Melanie asked.

Carl shook his head. "I don't know. I thought if they had me, they wouldn't need Michael."

Melanie's eyes narrowed. "Are you telling me you were . . . their thrall?"

Carl said stonily, "It was easier than being a meal."

Melanie shook her head. She couldn't judge Carl for that. He had done what was necessary to survive, with little hope. Plus, it meant he thought he was helping Michael. At least there was that.

She explained to him what she'd heard on the phone call. They didn't talk about Lara, and Carl didn't ask her about the other two male wolves who had come to help.

Melanie wondered if their mate bond could survive these secrets and infidelities. It seemed so weak . . . like cracked ceramic.

They heard crackling of leaves in the forest. Melanie turned toward the sound and said, "Just a minute."

She wanted a second to cover up, before Jean and Danver returned. Or to go back to bipedal wolf form, so her human breasts and ass weren't out.

But instead, she heard a cold, harsh voice from the woods, say, "No, I'm afraid your time has run out."

A dead, gaunt face stepped out of the forest. The vampires had found them.

DANVER

anver was totally focused on hunting down breakfast. It was the only way he could control his jealousy and concern. There were many reasons he didn't want to leave Carl alone with Melanie, but by diving completely into his wolf form, and keeping his attention on the natural rhythms of the hunt, it was possible to distract himself. Just.

He was even starting to enjoy the adrenaline rush and the exercise, when he was stopped in his tracks. His brain was abruptly torn from the hunt and any thought, other than Melanie. He could hear her voice as if she was whispering in his ear. It was even closer than that. It was in the animal part of his brain, echoing with an irresistible pull. Melanie was calling for him. Without a second's hesitation, he turned around completely and left behind the hunt. His alpha had called for him.

In his wolf form, his animal sense alight, he realized how right Jean was. It felt so right to follow Melanie's orders and come to her aid. He loved her. He respected her. And he realized he would follow her to Hell and back.

When he neared the clearing where they'd set up camp, he realized he *was* walking into Hell. Deadly vampires surrounded Melanie and

Carl – no fewer than five were closing in. Jean was right behind Danver. Danver wondered if he had heard the call as well, or if he'd been paying attention to Danver and simply followed him when he'd taken off back toward camp.

He didn't have much time to consider the mystery that was Jean the Vampire Hunter., because Jean didn't take any time to contemplate the scene in front of them. He leaped from the brush at the nearest vampire.

The vamp fell underneath Jean's attack and screamed. It slashed back at Jean, but the wolf had a good grip on its neck and tore at its torso. This distracted the four other vamps, giving Melanie and Carl enough time to transform into their wolf forms.

Except Carl didn't shift. He fell to his knees and put his hands up in his human form.

Danver stifled the urge to growl. He knew he should follow Jean's lead and that required the element of surprise.

Melanie immediately jumped into combat with one of the distracted vampires. But before Melanie could lock in combat, the vampire laughed and gestured with her hands. The impact of the hand gesture blew Melanie backward into a tree, which splintered from the impact of her wolf weight.

Danver jumped out and in one well-aimed leap, he clamped his mouth around the spellcasting vampire's outstretched hands. She screamed as he wrenched at her flesh.

Another vampire came to the spellcaster's aid, tearing at Danver. Danver felt his flesh dropping away from his body from the vampire's swipes. His regenerative abilities weren't able to keep up with the carnage.

But Danver knew everything was lost if the magic user was able to launch more spells. He was surprised she didn't knock everyone out with her first blow. He wondered if she could only direct it at one person at a time.

But he'd thought wrong. He'd assumed Melanie had been knocked out from the slam against the wood. He heard her howl as she lunged at the vampire who was assaulting his torso.

The magic-using vampire looked into Danver's eyes and hissed, "Foul dog." Then she said some words in a language he didn't understand, but it made his heart drop anxiously out of his chest into his stomach.

She spat on him. It got into his eye and burned. It burned as if someone had stabbed his eye with a red-hot poker. He roared. Screamed, really, but he kept his jaw clamped shut. He didn't let go, even as the poison from her spit tore out his eye's flesh.

At least Jean and Melanie had managed to incapacitate or keep the others busy. His body was healing his torso where the vampire had torn him open. His eye wasn't healing, though. It was dissolving in his skull from the vampire's spit. It was the most violent physical pain he'd ever experienced.

He felt Melanie nearby. She was safe, as long as he kept his mouth clamped. He could feel strength and power flowing from Melanie into him, and that pack bond and love helped him ignore the mounting pain.

The magic vampire kept chanting and taunting him. He felt his consciousness flickering and threatening to black out. He decided she must need her hands for long-range attacks, but if she was touching you already, she didn't need to direct the magic. She could just use the chants without pointing them or doing whatever the hell it was she did with her hands when she cast.

One of the vampires had broken away from the fight with Jean and Melanie. Danver could feel it standing over him, on the side of his face with the melted eye. Danver felt an unrestrained rage at Carl for his submission. If he had jumped into the fight and helped at all, then Danver wouldn't have his current wounds or be in this vulnerable position. Plus, the strengthened pack bond told him that Melanie was hurt too, although she was still moving and fighting well.

Danver didn't have much time to blame Carl, because in the next second, his whole back lit up in pain. The vampire had stabbed Danver with a silver knife. It didn't go in too deeply, but the horrible feeling of the silver branched out all through his body like an electric shock. His muscles clenched and he wished he could take off his muscles and skin and leave them behind. They brought too much pain as they rebelled and protested against the invading silver object.

The vampire with the knife shouted, "Let her go, or I kill you."

Danver was a good guy. He generally liked to do as people asked.

So he decided to do what the vampire asked. But not without taking his proverbial pound of flesh.

With the last bit of his strength and a wrenching twist, he tore the magic vampire's hands off of her body. She screamed as sluggish, coagulated blood dribbled out of her wrist stumps.

The vampire with the knife tried to plunge it in more deeply, but Danver pulled away with the knife still in his flesh. If it remained there too long, it would poison and kill him. But at least the vampire wouldn't be able to twist it into one of his vital organs.

It wasn't necessarily the case that silver killed werewolves. It only stopped their natural regeneration abilities. It burned like hell though, because it strangled the magic working in a werewolf's cells, so it couldn't work any healing miracles. If that went on for too long, the werewolf's body would shut down. Danver didn't know how long he had. He had to get someone to take the knife out of his upper back.

He couldn't risk shifting to remove it himself. If he shifted, part of the silver might break off and end up somewhere inside him. Then he'd be absolutely screwed. The only chance was if a human hand grabbed the knife and removed it in one piece. Even after that, Danver would need some rest to recover from the result of the silver working on his system.

The magic vampire with no hands screamed and disappeared. She either had teleportation or invisibility abilities. She was truly scary. The vampire who had stuck the knife into Danver pulled out two more. Undoubtedly, they were also silver. Danver took a quick second to survey the battlefield.

Carl still knelt in the middle of the field, naked and crying in a blubbering wail. Pathetic.

Jean was facing off against two vampires. He'd mutilated one of the five too badly for it to move. That vampire moaned and waited for its magic to reform it enough to walk or run away.

The two vampires had silver necklaces and bracelets, which strengthened their already powerful swings at Jean. But they were going for hand-to-hand combat. Danver was surprised, until he saw their unbelievable skill and speed.

Clearly, the vampires had combat specialties as werewolves dis. Jean's fighting style was based on agility and careful swipes. He looked self-possessed and choreographed, even as he parried and dodged the vampire's blows. It was strange to watch such a huge canine form dance so beautifully and enact such violence. The vampires were fast, but Jean was a touch faster. Something to remember in case he and Danver were ever on the opposite sides of a battle: there was no beating Jean with speed.

Melanie's fighting style was bolder. It had all the grace of a nuclear bomb. She threw herself into the fight with violence, and avoided hits with raw, powerful ducks and rolls.

The vampire she was fighting had brass knuckles lined with silver. He also threw silver stars on occasion, when he thought he saw an opening. Danver noticed with relief that she had avoided them so far.

Now it was Danver and the knife-wielding vampire. He could feel Melanie's grief, over the pack bond. She was sorry she was too busy with her own vamp to come and help Danver or to remove the knife. Danver wondered why she didn't force Carl into the battle. He was pack, too, and would need to respond to her call.

But Carl was still crying in fear and shaking on the ground with his hands up in a pose of surrender. Danver supposed that answered his question. Carl would be worthless in the fight, if he was forced to participate.

Danver circled carefully, keeping the vampire in front of him. He maneuvered so the rest of the fight was in front of him, as well, thus minimizing the chance that one of the other vampires would switch their target to him and cause more damage.

The vampire swirled his knives around in an impressive display of skill. It was so fast, Danver had a hard time following the twists and turns of the knives. The vampire thought Danver was distracted and defensive. With a barely perceptible flick of his wrist, he sent one of the knives toward Danver's face.

Danver's attention and reflexes were keenly calibrated to notice any sudden move, and he was able to duck underneath the flying silver knife. In the same motion, he ran forward, hoping to surprise and overwhelm the vampire before he could lash out again.

The vampire was ready for him. It flipped in the air, slashing out with the knife as Danver ran under him rather than into him. Danver was too low for the vampire's strike, and when the vampire landed on its feet and they both turned. They were unscathed.

Danver felt his legs weaken. He tried to steady himself but they shook.

The vampire taunted, "Ah, little puppy. So weak. Does it burn, puppy? I could make the burning stop."

He pulled one of the silver knives out of the tree behind him with a great twist. Danver cursed himself for letting the vamp get near his knife again. The vampire wielded both knives and twirled them like a terrible wheat thresher. He moved toward Danver with an equal measure of agility and power.

Danver's legs quivered no matter how much he tried to school them into standing straight. His bloodstream burned from the silver's poison. It was weakening his muscles and draining his consciousness.

He steadied himself for the vampire's unrelenting onslaught. But then a horrible, banshee-like scream broke through the clearing. It was a terrible sound – the advent of death.

Danver and his assailant both turned toward the sound.

DANVER

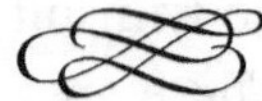

*I*n the midst of the battle, Jean had shifted into his bipedal wolf form and had torn a tree trunk out of the ground. He'd skewered two vampires with the trunk.

One was unconscious and his body rag-dolled, his torso totally split in half by the tree. Did that mean he was dead? Danver remembered Jean saying wooden stakes would kill a vampire.

But would a whole tree through the chest do it? Jean had said that vampires disintegrates into dust when they were "put down" (Jean's words for re-killing them). The vampire was unconscious and dribbling blood, but it wasn't disintegrating.

The other was the source of the horrible screams. He was very much awake and aware of every agonizing second he was impaled on the tree.

So a tree to the torso won't kill a vampire. Noted.

Having effectively and horrifyingly dealt with those two, Jean turned toward the remaining two vampires. He shifted into human form, which was ballsy. Danver was surprised he felt he had the upper hand enough to do that. Danver didn't feel as if he had the upper hand. Danver felt as if he was about to die.

The vampire with knives hissed and snarled at Jean. Jean said calmly, "Very dumb to fight in a forest. A wooden stake is not hard to make."

The vampire hissed, "Stupid to ally yourself with someone who owes us. You male werewolves are all so stupid. You'll do anything for your dumb pack bond. Well, this female is going to get you hunted down and killed like the dogs you are."

Danver growled. Even if he was a few seconds away from passing out, he wasn't about to let anybody insult Melanie.

The vampire continued, "There are many in our hive. As long as there is even one left, they will make more. You owe us. Your child." He slashed through the air, pointing his knife at Melanie. "Your child will be ours to play with."

Melanie roared. It was such a beautiful, powerful sound that Danver felt happy, despite his pain.

Keeping his eyes on the two remaining vampires, whose eyes were flickering between Jean and their impaled fellows, Jean meandered over to Danver.

As he moved, he said, "You come for this pack, we kill you. Simple. It is not the first time a werewolf pack had enemies."

He put on a little velvet glove, clean and white, which looked utterly shocking to Danver. How the hell had he managed to keep it clean this whole time? Where was the glove when he shifted?

With the glove on his hand, Jean wrenched the silver blade out of Danver. Danver whimpered gratefully and collapsed to the ground, the release from the pain shocking his system more than the pain itself had.

Danver eyed the vampires and tried to look as if he was only getting into a pouncing position. Jean patted his head, which would usually have annoyed Danver; but, honestly, at the moment he needed any support he could get.

Jean said, "Your claim to the boy exists only as long as this wolf does." Jean pointed at Carl with his silver knife in his gloved hand. He walked up to Carl and held the knife to his shaking throat. Carl squeaked in fear and begged, "Melanie, help!"

Melanie growled and lunged toward Jean, who said quickly, "Uh-

uh. Nobody move. No vampire, no werewolf. Nobody make the slightest move. Everybody stay still, until I finish saying my piece, or I slice him open."

Melanie stood still. Danver wondered again why she didn't order Jean to drop the knife, using pack bonds. Maybe Jean wasn't pack? They'd hunted and fought together. That usually inducted a member into the bonds, unless they rejected the association.

Perhaps Melanie wanted to see what Jean was planning before she made sure he didn't kill Carl. Or maybe her patience for her mate had run out.

Jean spoke slowly but brightly, as if he was talking to children who were fighting over a toy, "All the vampires will leave now. Go back home. Because if you don't, I'll kill this man outright. Then you'll have no right to take his son, because he won't be alive to agree to the deal. Not that I think you are anything other than ground-licking, dirt-sucking scum, for trading on the life of a gambling addict's first-born child. But I know your rules. The father or mother must consent to the thrall's servitude, if the thrall himself will not. I guarantee, the boy's mother will never, ever consent to such a life for him."

Melanie made a small, satisfied noise of assent, and then menaced the vampires with her dripping, sharp teeth. The vampires didn't pay her any attention. Their focus stayed locked on Jean and Carl.

Carl begged, "Please, for Chrissake, do what he says! Do what he says and take my son! Just leave me alone."

Jean looked at Carl in shock, as he blubbered.

Jean said, "You stupid bastard."

"We can take what we wanted all along, then," the vampire with the knives said triumphantly. "The father has agreed. Which means we no longer need him alive. We no longer need any of you."

Quick as a blink, the vampires disappeared into the forest. The two that were stuck through with a tree trunk were both unconscious. The screaming one finally passed out from the pain.

The wolves all shifted back to humans. With a single mind, they knew they had to talk through what just occurred.

Danver looked at the impaled forms and he could not help but feel sorry for them, after watching one writhe for so long. "They left their own, unconscious, with the enemy. No way to defend themselves."

Jean sneered. "Vampires like these don't care about each other. They join hives, but they don't have bonds as we do, or even as humans do. Vampires are together for their own sake, purely out of convenience. There is no pack mentality, which makes them very good at some things, but very bad at others."

Jean was still holding a knife to Carl's throat. Carl squeaked, "They left. Like you wanted. You can let go of me now."

Jean shrugged. "I am afraid I cannot let you go, until my alpha decides what to do with your traitorous, selfish hide."

Carl said, "Your alpha?"

Melanie burst toward him and grabbed him by the throat, pulling him to his feet. She was past anger, past hateful words. She looked him in the eye as her grip stayed tight around his neck.

Melanie said, "You gave your son's life to save your own. You didn't even have to do it. They would've left because otherwise Jean would've killed you. You gave them the only trump card we had, the only thing keeping us alive. The only reason they didn't kill us, was that they needed consent to take Michael. You gave that to them. Now, they can kill us for trying to protect him."

Carl hazarded, "Michael is a grown man. He can protect himself."

Melanie snarled, "He's seventeen, you idiot. You couldn't protect yourself against the vampire hive. Yet, you expect our son to handle it all himself."

Jean chuckled. "He doesn't expect your son to be able to get away. He knows he's dedicated his son to a lifetime of thralldom. Your boy is healthy, strong . . . Could live to two hundred, three hundred years. That's three hundred years with the vampires doing anything they'd like to him."

Melanie tightened her grip on Carl's throat. Her face was less stern, though. It was melting as tears threatened to burst through.

"Did you know, this whole time, that'd he'd have to become a thrall?" she asked Carl with a small voice, as if she was the one being choked. "You never planned on paying them back?"

Carl looked around, as if something in the forest would save him or give him a better answer to the question than the truth. Melanie squeezed his throat tighter.

Gasping, he said, "Yes. I knew."

Melanie didn't relax her grip. She stepped closer to him and looked him in the eyes. Then she spoke the words every werewolf feared hearing in his lifetime.

"Carl, I hereby break and disavow our mate bond. You are no longer my partner in life. I will no longer defend you to the death. You are cast away from me, and cast away from our pack. We offer you no defense; no friendship, no security, and we expect to receive none in return from you." She said the last part with extra venom. It was true. The pack had never expected Carl to be there for them.

Now it was official. She let go of Carl and he slumped to the ground. Jean still had the silver knife in his hand as they waited for Carl's reaction.

Carl said in disbelief, "You can't do that. I'm still in the pack. You can't kick me out."

Melanie spoke with a power in her voice that made Danver stand up a little straighter, "I can. It's my right and responsibility as alpha."

When she said that magic word, Jean and Danver smiled, though in very different ways. Jean looked as if he had watched a great joke play out to the end. Danver smiled for genuine joy at Melanie accepting what was truly meant to be her role.

Jean said with mock sadness, "Oh, how disappointing for you, Carl. And how frightening. You see, you may not know this, if you've always been in a pack, but werewolves with no pack . . . No one to avenge them should they die . . . They're open season for supernatural hunters."

Jean poked Carl in the back with his knife. It was only a bump, but the pinprick of pain caused Carl to jump in the air and run toward Melanie.

She put up a hand to stop him. She said, "If you touch me, I'll tear your hands off." Less stern, she shook her head and gave Carl a sorrowful look. "We made a miracle together. Then you threw it away.

That's unforgivable. Any slight to me, any damage to our relationship, I could've taken. Hell, I would've found the $800,000. I would've worked for it and stolen it and scrounged it up from the depths of the ocean floor, however I could figure it out. But, you gave them *our son*. You betrayed our pup. For that . . . you're lucky I'm only expelling you."

The fire in her eyes replaced any sympathy she had shown earlier. Even Carl knew there was no chance to beg his way out. What he had done was forever marked on his soul.

"I don't have any money. I don't have any clothes," Carl said. He looked around at all three of the people surrounding him with his hands out.

Jean clapped him on the shoulders with a friendly air. "Then you best get running. The hunters could come any second, and you'll want to at least have some underwear to shit, when they show up."

Carl looked at him with unshakable fear. He saw he was getting no sympathy from either of the other two faces. He looked at Danver, who arranged his features to express exactly how much he wanted to tear Carl's limbs off.

Shaking, naked, and scared, Carl turned into the woods and began to run. He shifted into a true wolf form, as he went. It was much smaller than the usual werewolf wolf form, and was mainly used for sneaking or covert operations.

Melanie didn't look at him as he left. She looked to Jean and asked, "Are the vampires going to come after my pup now?"

Jean nodded, looking uncharacteristically but appropriately worried. "I am afraid they will be on their way already."

Melanie nodded in return. She looked at Danver to make sure she had his agreement. "Then we're wasting time. We've got to get home and warn them."

She looked off into the trees, suddenly arrested by a thought. "This was all a waste of time," she said softly, almost too quietly for Danver to hear.

"We don't have to get home to warn them," Danver said.

Melanie looked at him with a lifted eyebrow. "You've got a phone hidden somewhere?"

Jean put his finger up in a eureka moment. "Ah-ha! He is right. The alpha can pull pack bonds. You can't give the full story. But you can order Wes to escape, run, etcetera."

She said, "I don't know . . . I don't really know how to do it. Every time I've done it so far has been an accident."

Danver walked up and took Melanie by the hand.

He said, "It's Wes, your brother. He's been there for you your whole life. At least, you've been there for him." Melanie smirked at that. Danver continued, "Call him in a way you both know. He'll understand."

Melanie smiled for the first time in days. Danver smiled himself, feeling pleased at her joy. His smile muscles felt out of practice.

Melanie closed her eyes, unnecessary but helpful to focus. She whispered, "Wes. Rabbit hole."

She popped her eyes back open after a moment, surprised to have felt such a strong answer. She said, "We used to tell each other that, when our parents came home and they were angry. It meant hide whatever you were doing because you were going to get your ass kicked. He heard me . . . All the way in New Mexico. I could feel it. He knows something has gone wrong and he's taking the family to hide."

She squeezed Danver's hand and looked him deeply in the eye.

She said, "This alpha shit is kind of scary."

Danver squeezed her hand back. "Not if it's in the hands of the right person."

Jean clapped. "This is all very adorable and you two are a lovely nude sculpture I simply must carve sometime, but we must be going."

In a moment, the clearing was empty, except for the echoes of howls getting further and further away.

MELANIE

As they rushed toward the part of New Mexico they called home, Melanie couldn't get a horrible question out of her mind. How had the vampires found them?

They were all running naked and fully shifted into wolves. They'd left behind any electronics that could have given the vampires any signal. They were deep in the mountains before they even stopped running.

Vampires are fast, but there's no way they could have kept up with them and tracked them that far through the mountains, with none of the werewolves noticing. That meant the only way they could have tracked them was with magic.

How could the magic user have tracked them so far? Melanie realized she should have asked Jean before they took off, but she guessed it didn't matter. Even if they were able to track them from that distance, if the werewolves got enough of a head start, it didn't matter.

They were running straight home, anyway. The vampires were going after her son. The first place they'd look would be the house on the ranch. The werewolves had to be able to get there first. Wes, Cassidy, and the pups would be holed up somewhere and hidden, but if the vampires made it into the ranch house, they might search the place and track the family. If Danver, Melanie, and Jean got home first, they could remove any trace that they had ever lived there and run for the hills.

If they didn't get there before the vampires, they'd have to race them to the hideout. Wherever Wes had chosen. Melanie was carefully not pulling on Wes, to find out where he went, in case Marwenn's magic tracking could follow the pack bond.

Melanie kept a close hold on Jean and Danver. She noticed, with confused feelings, that the pack bond with Jean was strong. She wondered if Danver had noticed, or if she had to accept Jean into the pack formally, before he'd be able to communicate over the bond with the other members.

She didn't know how she felt about him joining the pack. He was a valuable ally, for sure. But now that she was free from Carl . . . she wondered what would happen between her and Danver.

She couldn't spend too much time on this. She had to try to navigate them home. They'd ended up in Arizona and gotten some clothes and directions, so she knew they were at least in New Mexico by now.

She was less confident about honing in on home without anybody at the house. She'd figured it would be simple to find the ranch house, because she could just feel out Wes once they got close enough. That wasn't an option anymore.

As they got into desert that felt a little more familiar, Melanie fell back so Danver could take point. He was a more skilled tracker and more used to the desert surrounding the house. He took up his position quickly, his nose and ears alert.

Melanie and Jean followed close behind. Melanie watched Danver's strong haunches as he bounded in front of them at breakneck speed. His thighs were thick and twitched with latent power, even with all the pressure and speed he was pumping out of them.

Melanie wondered what it would be like to rut with him in full wolf form. Carl had never wanted to. He only preferred her human form. But Melanie had always been curious . . . What would it be like to be plowed under by a strong wolf thrust? What would the sensation be, to be in human form and attacked, mounted, and taken by a wolf cock?

Melanie didn't have any more time to think it over, because suddenly they burst through the sparse forest and into a large clearing. Not too far off, she could see a cute adobe home. They'd arrived at the ranch.

Melanie didn't shift out of wolf form. She wanted to be ready to fight if there were vampires here already. She looked at Jean. He sniffed the air and held very still, moving a little closer to the house. Then he opened his eyes, breathed deeply, and shook his wolf head at Melanie.

She shifted into human form as she ran toward the house. The two men followed suit, close behind her. When they reached the door, they found it locked, but it took only one kick from Melanie to burst it open. She whipped around to the men as the three of them entered.

She said, "Destroy everything that could help them track us or find out anything about Wes and Cassidy. We can only pray they didn't do their full research on the entire pack; they seemed focused on my family. But we don't want to leave anything behind that could help them."

With a look out of the side of his eye, Jean said, "It is a difficult request. We might miss something."

Melanie said, "Yes. That's why we'll go through the house once, get anything valuable that the pack needs, and destroy anything that could give us away. Then we'll burn the house down."

Danver looked at Melanie with wide eyes. He looked around the loved, adorably-decorated home they'd enjoyed together for over a year now.

He whispered to Melanie, "Are you sure?" The thought of tearing down the ranch home made his heart break. He said, "What about when we come back?"

Melanie said firmly, "A house can be rebuilt. People can't be replaced. If the vampires have any clues to find us, at all, they will find us. They will kill us and take Michael."

Danver shook his head. "Carl was expelled from the pack. Doesn't that remove his right to offer Michael?"

Jean explained what Melanie had intuited. "He already gave his consent. As far as the vampires are concerned, they believe they own Michael, now. There's no way to reverse it. The deal is done. The die is cast. Whatever metaphor you prefer, there is no way to stop them. You can only hide or kill the whole hive."

Danver snarled, "Maybe that's what we should be doing, then."

Jean said diplomatically, "Perhaps. But until we can figure out how big the hive is, who is loyal to it, how many states it stretches over, etcetera, it may be better to hide while we do our reconnaissance."

Danver didn't respond. He understood the logic of that, even if he didn't like it. Melanie appreciated his hardline sense of right and wrong. Danver would never have sold out the pack for any benefit to himself. Melanie was hit by a very big wish to have met Danver a couple decades ago, before she met Carl.

Oh, well. You can't erase the past. You can only make better choices in the future.

Melanie said, "So we're settled. Get to work."

Danver rushed toward the stairs, to start with the upper floor, but Jean held still. He was frozen, like a statue. He shifted quickly into wolf form and smelled the air.

He growled. Melanie didn't need a translation.

She shifted and Danver did, too. They were just in time for the crash through the window. A small round shape landed in the middle of the house.

Melanie leaped behind the dining table and kicked it over. It was thick, solid, well-treated wood. She hoped it would deflect enough of the bomb's force that she would still be able to fight after it went off. But it wasn't a regular bomb. It was a smoke bomb. The house filled up with it until Melanie could barely see.

She wondered if Danver and Jean had gotten out before it went off. She hoped they had. Right now, she was in a vulnerable position, and nearly blinded in the middle of the kitchen area. She remembered that Danver had alluded to military service before, and Jean was definitely used to combat. That gave her a burst of optimism that helped her forget the anxiety of her present predicament.

The first thing was to get away from the smoke and get out of the house. Then she could regroup with Danver and Jean and attack whoever was attacking them. Except she felt a presence near her. It was not one of her wolves. It was an enemy, and either it was wearing a gas mask or vampires didn't need to see or breathe in the usual way.

Melanie really despised the undead at this point. She remembered how carefully Jean always said, "Some vampires . . ." instead of making it sound as if they were all this nasty and evil. But after this experience, she'd have trouble trusting humans in a fake vampire costume, much less real vamps.

She could feel the vampire's eyes on her, with her hunter senses, even if she couldn't see. She was sure they had something nasty planned for her. She didn't give them the chance. She lunged toward where the staring came from. She missed it, but only just.

She heard the vamp bump into the dining table. She knew where the front door was, in relation to the table. She didn't need to see to move around her own home. She swiped at the vampire with her hefty paw, and it rolled away from her with a hiss. She took off running toward the front door.

She felt the air displaced right behind her legs. The vampire had swiped a knife at her, but she was a millimeter too fast. In a second, she was out the front door.

She blinked her eyes and breathed the night air deeply to cleanse her lungs. She couldn't see Danver or Jean, but she felt them. She took off for Danver in a shed nearby.

When she got there, she noticed that Jean and Danver had shifted back to human form. They were grabbing cans of gasoline that were usually used to fuel the tractor or other ranch vehicles.

Jean said with a grin, waving his hand toward the gasoline like an elegant magician, "Given the change in circumstances, we figured our alpha would not mind if we skipped to Step Three of the plan."

Danver said with heat, "Let's burn them to the ground, Melanie."

She took only a second to consider it. Then she nodded.

Jean and Danver shifted into bipedal wolf form while Melanie took up position at the front door. It was the only entrance and exit out of the house.

Quickly, the men poured out the gasoline. Danver lit the flame with a match he'd found, but only after Melanie had given him a final nod.

All three wolves took up positions on the different sides of the house. The vampires must have wanted them to run away, so they could look through the house in peace. They were about to get anything but peace. Melanie would be able to surprise attack any that came out the front door. The same for any that jumped out of a window.

Even if they got away from the werewolves, it didn't matter. As long as they weren't able to gain intel on the family or their current whereabouts.

The fact the vampires had risked coming here showed they weren't tracking Melanie, magically or otherwise. If they were tracking her, they could've just waited for her to join up with the rest of the pack, then followed her and found the rest of the family that way. They must've been tracking Carl, when they found them in the woods. Melanie once again cursed the day she'd ever met Carl.

Except if she hadn't, she wouldn't have Michael. Again, she realized how good it was we couldn't reverse the past. Because in our anger, we'd lose the good, along with the bad.

She watched the flames burst and begin to devour her family's home. She waited for the chance to punish those responsible.

DANVER

Most of the vampires got away, but the werewolves did a nasty number on one or two. More importantly, they preserved the family's safety, by keeping their information from the vampires.

After the flames died down, they sifted through the ash. They destroyed anything they found that wasn't already demolished. It was a strange, sad feeling, but necessary.

Afterwards, Danver assumed they would start their hunt for Wes and Cassidy's hiding spot with the pups. But Melanie didn't move. She stood at the edge of the woods, watching the rubble of their former lives. When she noticed him staring at her, she said, "I want to make sure they don't come back. And that they aren't tracking me. I'm pretty sure they followed Carl, when he was with us. But if we wait here overnight . . ."

She trailed off. Danver understood. She wanted to make sure the job was done for now.

He walked up and stood beside her. She looked at him, looking more scared than he had possibly ever seen her look. A genuine vulnerability filled her face.

"Whatever needs to be done, we will do it. The pack will be safe," Danver said softly.

She smiled. Danver was embarrassed, suddenly, standing beside her beautiful form entirely naked. Now that there was no immediate threat to life and limb, he could feel the usual heat he felt from her form.

She reached out and grabbed his hand. She squeezed it tightly, turning herself to face him.

He heard Jean walking toward them, but when he saw the two holding hands in the moonlight, he turned around and strolled off.

"I'll just make the rounds and take my turn guarding, huh?" he said casually, before he walked away from them, whistling a song happily.

Danver felt utterly lost in Melanie's eyes. When she smiled in the way he loved best, lighting up her whole face, he couldn't help but step closer to her.

She said, "I'm free now, Danver. To choose whom I want. To choose a good man."

But something remained in her face that held on to her doubt. Danver looked at her intently, wanting to root it out so she could let it go. He wanted her so badly.

"I'm not asking anything," she said with a choking noise. "I'm not requesting anything. In this moment, I'm a woman. Not your alpha." She let go of him and held her hands at her side.

She looked into his face: utterly vulnerable, completely honest. "What do you want, Danver?" she asked.

He wrapped his hands underneath the luscious curve of her ass and fell onto the forest floor on top of her. She squealed with joy.

He kissed her. The heat and wetness of her mouth reminded him of how good it felt inside of her pussy. Their tongues caressed each other gently, while their lips and bodies rubbed against each other vigorously.

He pulled back only long enough to say, "I love you, Melanie."

She said, "I love you, Danver."

Unable to control himself anymore, after hearing that, he thrust himself inside of her. She breathed deeply with the shock of his huge member entering her, and then she screamed and howled underneath his powerful thrusts. He kept his huge hands clenched on her ass cheeks, squeezing them and pushing her hips upward to meet his powerful thrusts. She felt completely taken and helpless under the wonderful power of his love and desire.

As she screamed and moaned from his cock repeatedly punching her insides, he whispered and cried out her name, and his love for her. Hearing him say, "I love you, Melanie," was so sweet, and when coupled with the brilliant pleasure and pain of his cock's onslaught, it brought her to an elated state of heightened joy.

She wanted to be touching him as much as possible. She wrapped her legs and arms around him, gripping him tightly as he rocked her frame with his lust. She bit into his shoulder, wanting to taste him, to have as much of him inside her as possible.

She flicked her tongue over his neck and bit him repeatedly, not drawing blood, but leaving pink indents in his hard skin. He shouted and roared as she did this, finally unable to take the heightened feeling.

He flipped her over. She screamed, "Yes, yes!" over and over, excited for him to take her completely. He shoved her face into the dirt with a growl and pulled up her ass.

It was not long before they reached climax. Screaming together, howling into the night, he bent over to hug her torso as they convulsed. He came deep inside her. The burning warmth of his semen added more pleasure to the pulsing of her orgasm.

They held each other like this in the quiet of the forest for a while. Melanie laughed a bit, needing some way for the joy to escape her elated brain. Danver breathed deeply and inhaled her scent with unbridled joy.

From a far distance away, Jean shouted, "No intruders on the perimeter!" He was too far away to see them, so he was announcing his presence to the pair so they could recover themselves.

For the first time ever, Danver realized he kind of liked Jean. At least, the guy was considerate about giving two mates their alone time.

Danver pulled out of Melanie. She sighed happily, as her pussy released him. They tried their best to wipe off with nearby leaves, but Danver's semen still dripped out from Melanie and down her leg.

Jean walked into the clearing with a grin. He said, "It would appear I must inform the Paranormal True Mate Dating Agency that I have not been selected as mate."

Melanie grinned. "Sorry Jean. Thanks for your help, though. I'm afraid we'll have to ask for your help, still."

He put up a hand, shaking away any praise. "I feel attached to your pack," he said. "It is hard to hunt and kill with someone and not become attached. If you will have me, I would love to be a member, even though I will not have a mate." He nodded respectfully to Danver, who appreciated the firm clarification.

Danver liked how well Jean was taking this, and how firmly he was reiterating that he would not consider himself a rival. Maybe Jean was an old-fashioned kind of guy after all.

Melanie said, "I approve. But before we make it official, we'll need to talk to Wes, Cassidy, and Michael. Make sure they approve of the new entry, as well."

Jean shrugged. "I like you. I would like to help you all survive the vampire's attempts at vengeance. It's up to you whether you accept that or not."

Melanie laughed. "Great point. I'm sure Wes will like you, and Cassidy will appreciate what you've done for us."

Danver said, "Cassidy manages to like Wes, and he's more annoying than Jean. I'm sure we'll all get along fine."

Jean laughed at that and smiled at Danver. It was actually a friendly, sincere smile. He looked genuinely pleased that Danver had stopped hating him.

"When should we take off toward the rest of the pack, then?" Jean said to Melanie, serious and business-like again.

She thought for a second. Danver appreciated how she considered things before jumping into decisions. He'd seen alphas make all of their moves purely on impulse, and it never turned out well in the long-run. She closed her eyes. She felt along the pack bonds. Danver could feel the ripple as she located Wes.

She opened her eyes in a flash and laughed; her smile lighting up her face brilliantly. She said, "That asshole."

Danver and Jean waited for an explanation, with various levels of amusement. Jean hadn't been around long enough to understand how annoying Wes's constant joking was.

Melanie shook her head in disbelief, but she clearly thought Wes was being funny and she was at least a little entertained. "I don't know where he's got Cassidy and the baby. Somewhere nearby, where he can keep his mate bond open with Cassidy and feel her out."

Jean said, "I thought humans can't feel bonds."

Danver explained, "There's still a magic connection that their mates can tap into."

Jean nodded in understanding. Melanie continued, "So he's got them in a hotel somewhere or a motel or something. But he and Michael . . ." She laughed, "He's such an ass. I used to hate haunted houses when I was little. Not literal ones. Like, the scary corn-field mazes or the fake homes where costumed humans or animatronics leap out at you? I was jumpy as a kid, and I didn't control my shift well. So I'd get scared, and worry the whole time I'd shift."

Danver said, "He's in a haunted house?"

Melanie rolled her eyes. "There's one in Santa Fe. A corn-field maze. He and Michael are hiding in plain sight as werewolves. It's stupid. But there are robot werewolves in that maze. Wes destroyed the robot and took its place."

Jean cracked the hell up. He wiped a tear from his eyes and said, "That's bleeding brilliant. So people walk out of the corn maze going, 'Wow, what a realistic werewolf,' and the people who set up the corn maze say, 'Thank you for enjoying the maze!' and nobody is any the wiser. The vampires sure as hell wouldn't look for them there."

Melanie nodded, stifling a laugh. "Yes, because what werewolf is stupid enough to pretend to be an animatronic?"

Danver said, "It's dangerous. What if they get found out?"

Jean said, "How could they? Who is going to go through the maze and realize that it was a real werewolf, and not a robot or man in a mask? It's fool-proof."

Danver sneered. "Because he's a fool."

Melanie smiled and grabbed his hand. "Interested in getting spooked? I know a great corn maze in Santa Fe."

MELANIE

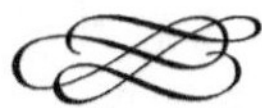

Melanie's cocktail glistened in the mid-afternoon sun. It sparkled like jewels and tasted like firecrackers. She looked around the beach. Michael was playing with his little cousin and actually cracking a smile or two. It was too hard, even for him, not to enjoy the perfectly warm sand and crystal-clear water.

Cassidy sipped daintily at her drink as she sunbathed beside Melanie. Cassidy said, "I never thought that going into hiding would taste so good."

Melanie laughed and said, "It does on the French Riviera."

When the pack had reunited, they'd celebrated everyone coming out of the most recent crises safely. Cassidy was shocked and saddened when she heard about her ranch, but she understood why they'd had to burn it down and why they would all have to leave. She had known that that life was not going to be simple or normal, when she married a werewolf.

Melanie sat up straighter and looked into Cassidy's eyes with all the empathy and apology she rightly deserved. She said to her sister-in-law, "I'm sorry about the ranch."

Cassidy sighed, but then she smiled and gestured. "Early retirement isn't so bad. Wes and Davie love it." Wes played volleyball against Danver and Jean. None of the men wanted to be on the same team, so they were playing a weird three-way version.

Whenever Cassidy looked at her pup or her mate, her smile deepened and her shoulders relaxed. She said sincerely, "I'm glad everyone is safe, and thanks to Jean, we got to hide somewhere beautiful."

Once the pack had reconvened, they'd started their research into the hive that was after them. It was bigger than they thought. Hundreds of vampires answered to the Ancient One at the top of the hive's heap, and the hive's power crossed much of the western US, even as far east as Chicago.

Suddenly, the United States felt like a very small country, with nowhere to hide. Before the pack could feel too much despair, Jean revealed the tiniest bit of information about himself.

He had friends in Europe, particularly France. They could help transport and hide the family.

Nobody was sure what the next step was for the family. They didn't think they could hide forever in a resort on the French Riviera. But they needed time to think, heal, and figure out their priorities.

Melanie was reluctant to launch any counterattacks or even come out of hiding until Davie was old enough to defend himself. She knew her ex-mate's stupid choices had unfairly put Cassidy's pup at risk, as well. She felt the most sorry about that.

She'd felt bad about moving Michael again, but it turned out he loved France. He liked the French girls, and they thought his American accent and firm physique were incredibly . . . interesting. He got along much easier with the kids here than the kids back home.

So the only one who was hurt by this ordeal was Cassidy. Melanie couldn't let Cassidy's good nature forgive her just like that.

Melanie said softly, "But you'll lose the ranch, if we stay away too long. The rest of us are ghosts, we don't exist anyway. They'll declare you dead."

Cassidy smiled and said quickly, "Oh, is that what you're worried about? Listen, I bought that ranch to help the Mexican Wolf population in New Mexico. I have a provision in my will. I made it as soon as I bought the ranch. If I am to die or disappear, the whole property goes to the wolf rescue. I didn't want my bloodsucking family coming in and taking my land away from the people and animals that need and deserve it." She paused for a second and giggled. "Metaphorically, bloodsucking. I hope."

Melanie said with a smile, "So you're okay? The ranch will go to the wolf rescue and keep doing the good work you wanted it to?"

Cassidy nodded. "I'm sad I can't help out more. Saving the wolves was my life's mission. But, I've got new wolves now," she gestured at the pack playing in the sand and surf, "Taking care of you guys is a full-time job."

Melanie laughed. She took a deep sip of her cocktail, enjoying the remaining bubbles and the sting of the alcohol.

Cassidy said playfully, "So if you're alpha, do I have to do every-thing you say? Or is it just the wolves?"

Melanie shot her a look. "You don't have to do everything I say, no. Not only because you're human and can't tap into the pack bonds but also because you're the only one here, besides me, with an ounce of good sense."

Cassidy laughed happily. Melanie knew she didn't have any subor-dination to worry about from her sister-in-law. Cassidy was honest about how she felt and gave good guidance, but she respected Melanie. Plus, if Melanie ordered Cassidy to do something that she truly could not do or did not agree with, she didn't want her to feel compelled to do it. They trusted each other on a woman-to-woman level and Melanie wanted to keep it that way.

Being alpha was a strange feeling. It was not a common position for a woman. It was definitely tempting to make Wes do all the house chores, as compensation for being such a jerk for most of his life. But she knew the others would never have accepted her, and she wouldn't have even become alpha, if it wasn't the right thing for everyone. The pack bonds figured it out through the magic of the pack's interrela-tionships. Melanie realized she was the only one with a connection and understanding of everyone in the pack.

Jean had been her lover and had fought by her side on the battle-field, when everyone else was still a stranger to him. Wes was her brother, and he'd always recognized she had the better sense between the two of them. She had a bond with Cassidy as another woman and mother.

Michael was her son, of course, and then there was the pup Davie, whom she was helping to raise, could only say, "Mew," as her name. He couldn't quite nail the "l" noise but he was getting there.

Finally, there was one, with whom she was forever linked through a stronger mate bond than she had ever felt with Carl . . . Danver. The passion and love they felt for each other burned along the magic bonds so brightly that she felt always drawn toward him. Her gaze roved over him as he played volleyball.

The sun glistened off his wet abs. He felt her looking and turned to stare back at her.

The volleyball rocketed toward him. Without cutting off his gaze at Melanie, he put a hand up and caught the ball. Wes and Jean protested, but Danver tossed them the ball back and hustled toward Melanie.

Danver walked up and nodded at her drink. "You're almost done. You want another one?"

Melanie said, "You read my mind," giddy under his careful and loving attentions. She watched with pride as he walked toward the bar and other women on the beach checked out his incredible body.

Cassidy waved at Wes. She pointed at her drink.

He yelled back, "What? I'm about to win!"

She said, "I want another drink, you dope!"

"You can walk," he replied.

Cassidy looked at him with a dropped jaw. Melanie hooted with laughter as he ran over and said, "I'm sorry, sweetie. Please don't break up with me. Remember how much you love me?"

She said, "Yeah, yeah." He went to the bar, smiling and waving at her and blowing kisses.

Cassidy shook her head and Melanie said, "If you wanted someone well-behaved, you should've stuck with Danver."

Cassidy sighed and said, "Nah. Feels like everything turned out exactly as it should be."

As Melanie watched her beautiful pack, and the sun played in the sparkling waves, she knew she couldn't argue with that. Everything had turned out perfectly.

EPILOGUE: LARA

The vampire thrall held their breath as she knelt before the Ancient One. He circled her, loving the combined feeling of her adoration and fear.

Finally, he took his lanky, death-like frame and sat on his throne. With a wispy, croaking voice, he said "I can see why you are able to seduce so many. Your curves are delicious, your skin soft, your gentle trembling . . . nearly irresistible, and I've been dead for over a thousand years." He looked thoughtful for a moment. "Almost two thousand. Maybe over two thousand, now. It's hard to count when you're my age. Plus the calendars have changed."

He looked at the two vampires who had brought him the thrall.

"How many of the dogs has she managed to seduce into our service?" he asked.

Lara watched him from under her heavily mascaraed eyelashes. She felt a thrill of pride as the vampire behind her revealed, "We have her to thank for thirty-two werewolf thralls."

The Ancient One's eyebrows shot up. Well, more like crawled. He didn't make any movement particularly quickly.

"That is a large number for one human woman to bring to us," he said with satisfaction.

The other vampire that had brought her here, the magic-using female whose hands were growing back grotesquely, said sardonically, "She works fast."

The Ancient One looked at her hands with glee. "The vampire hunter, he did that to you?"

The magic user vampire responded with burning hatred, "No. One of his pack."

The Ancient One nodded and turned his attention back to Lara. He said, "You know, child, it is severely distressing to us that the most successful vampire hunter since the Great Violence drove us out of Europe has found a pack. He will be even more powerful now."

Lara felt her hate bubble up. She said, "I am sorry he escaped with his whore and her servants. They don't deserve to live. They deserve a horrifying death for going against your beautiful hive."

Her tears started to come. She knew vampires didn't like crying women, so she swallowed her tears. They didn't like to see humans display emotion, when they themselves couldn't manage it.

The Ancient One nodded and said with satisfaction, "You are truly loyal. You have taken over thirty men as lovers, and turned each of them over to us, for a lifetime of thralldom. Betrayed them all, for us."

"It's hardly a betrayal," Lara said with bright, wild eyes. "It's the only chance for a werewolf dog to live with any dignity. By serving the vampires, they live as they should: as pets to a higher being."

The Ancient One stood up and walked toward her, taking her chin in his hands. He asked her solemnly, "Do you consider yourself a pet of ours?"

She blinked up at him with her wide, seemingly-innocent eyes. She said, "I don't consider myself at all. I am only what you want me to be."

He looked at the vampires who'd brought her. They nodded, giving their assent as proof of her total devotion to the hive.

The Ancient One laughed and said, "None of my vampires have been able to kill the vampire hunter. He escapes our every attempt, and murders us at will. But perhaps, a human woman, so beautiful and ready to offer her body to the dogs . . . Perhaps you are better suited to defeat him."

Lara felt a wellspring of pride burst through her body. Finally, a chance to show her devotion truly to the hive and the majestic vampires.

She would find the vampire hunter. He would fall for her and her bodily charms. Then she would kill him in whatever way the hive desired.

Or even better, turn him into a thrall, as she had the others.

She said, "Yes, please," to the Ancient One, and as her response pleased him, he laughed deeply until it drove him into a coughing fit.

He smiled. "She will do quite well."

Lara smiled, too. She would kill the vampire hunter and the rest of his foolish pack.

They'd all die for disrespecting the hive.

I hope you enjoyed the second book in the Paranormal True Mate Dating Agency series! Thank you so much for reading. Wasn't it wonderful how Danver's love for Melanie survived all the turmoil and trouble they went through together? Their love conquered all!

Jean was such a gentleman to bow out when he did. But he won't be alone for long. The seductive and smart Lara is on his trail. Will sparks fly when they meet? To find out, you'll have to order the next book: "Assassin Wolf's Last Chance at Love" by clicking HERE.

Happy reading! I look forward to seeing you in the next romance with this sweet, loving werewolf pack.

THE END

9 798562 816818